KU-165-846

Praise for *Improvement*

'[A] love-and-loss story seasoned with single motherhood and smuggling schemes, National Book Award finalist Joan Silber's *Improvement* hits the sexy sweet spot from page one.'

Elle

'I love all of Joan Silber's work for her mastery of character, her ferocious and searching compassion, and her elegant lines that make the mind hum for hours.'

Lauren Groff

'Without fuss or flourishes, Joan Silber weaves a remarkably patterned tapestry connecting strangers from around the world to a central car accident. The writing here is funny and down-to-earth, the characters are recognizably fallible, and the message is quietly profound: We are not ever really alone, however lonely we feel.'

Wall Street Journal, top fiction titles of 2017

'An everyday masterpiece.'

Newsday

'An accomplished, wise, humane book, generously graced with those fleeting but vivid moments – of puzzlement, vexation and love – in which the humanity of her characters shines through.'

Colin Barrett

Also by Joan Silber

Improvement

Joan Silber

ALLEN&UNWIN

First published in Great Britain in 2019 by Allen & Unwin

First published in the United States in 2017 by Counterpoint

Allen & Unwin
c/o Atlantic Books
Ormond House
26–27 Boswell Street
London WC1N 3JZ
Phone: 020 7269 1610
Fax: 020 7430 0916
Email: UK@allenandunwin.com
Web: www.allenandunwin.com/uk

A CIP catalogue record for this book is available from the British Library.

Internal design by Wah-Ming Chang
Cover design by Marina Drukman

Hardback ISBN 978 1 91163 006 7
E-Book ISBN 978 1 76063 726 2

Printed and bound in Great Britain by TJ International Ltd.

10 9 8 7 6 5 4 3 2 1

For Myra,
with great thanks

Part I

I

Everyone knows this can happen. People travel and they find places they like so much they think they've risen to their best selves just by being there. They feel distant from everyone at home who can't begin to understand. They take up with beautiful locals, they settle in, they get used to how everything works, they make homes. But maybe not forever.

I had an aunt who was such a person. She went to Istanbul when she was in her twenties. She met a good-looking carpet seller from Cappadocia. She'd been a classics major in college and had many questions to ask him, many observations to offer. He was a gentle and intelligent man who spent his days talking to travelers. He'd come to think he no longer knew what to say to Turkish girls, and he loved my aunt's airy conversation. When her girlfriends went back to Greece, she stayed behind and moved in with him. This was in 1970.

His shop was in Sultanahmet, where tourists went, and

he lived in Fener, an old and jumbled neighborhood. Kiki, my aunt, liked having people over, and their apartment was always filled with men from her boyfriend's region and expats of various ages. She was happy to cook big semi-Turkish meals and make up the couch for anyone passing through. She helped out in the store, explained carpet motifs to anyone who walked in—those were stars for happiness, scorpion designs to keep real scorpions away. In her letters home, she sounded enormously pleased with herself—she dropped Turkish phrases into her sentences, reported days spent sipping *çay* and *kahve*. All this became lore in my family.

She wrote to her father, who suffered from considerable awkwardness in dealing with his children (her mother had died some six years before), and to her kid brother, who was busy hating high school. The family was Jewish, from a forward-thinking leftist strain; Kiki had gone to camps where they sang songs about children of all nations, so no one had any bigoted objections to her Turkish boyfriend. Kiki sent home to Brooklyn a carpet she said was from the Taurus Mountains. Her father said, "Very handsome colors. I see you are a connoisseur. No one is walking on it, I promise."

Then Kiki's boyfriend's business took a turn for the worse. There was a flood in the basement of his store and a bill someone never paid and a new shop nearby that was getting all the business. Or something. The store had to close. Her family thought this meant that Kiki was coming home at last. But, no. Osman, her guy, had decided to move back to the village he was from, to help his father, who raised pumpkins for their seed-oil. Also tomatoes, green squash, and eggplant. Kiki was up for the move; she wanted to see the real Turkey. Istanbul was really so Western now. Cappadocia was very ancient and she couldn't wait to see the volcanic rock. She was getting married! Her family in Brooklyn was surprised about that part. Were they invited to the wedding? Apparently not. In fact, it had already happened by the time they got the letter. "I get to wear a beaded hat and a glitzy headscarf, the whole shebang," Kiki wrote. "I still can't believe it."

Neither could any of her relatives. But they sent presents, once they had an address. A microwave oven, a Mister Coffee, an electric blanket for the cold mountains. They were a practical and liberal family, they wanted to be helpful. They didn't hear from Kiki for a while and her father worried that the gifts had been stolen in the mail. "I know it's hard for you to imagine," Kiki wrote, "but we do very well without electricity here. Every morning I make a wood fire in the stove. Very good-smelling smoke. I make a little fire at the bottom of the water heater too."

Kiki built fires? No one could imagine her as the pioneer wife. Her brother, Alan (who later became my father), asked what kind of music she listened to there and if she had a radio. She sent him cassette tapes of favorite Turkish singers—first a crappy male crooner and then a coolly plaintive woman singer who was really very good. Alan was always hoping to visit, but first he was in college and working as a house painter in the summers and then he had a real job in advertising that he couldn't leave. Kiki said not a word about making any visits home. Her father offered to pay for two tickets to New York so they could all meet her husband, but Kiki wrote, "Oh, Dad. Spend your money on better things." No one nagged her; she'd been a touchy teenager, given to sullen outbursts, and everyone was afraid of that Kiki appearing again.

She stayed for eight years. Her letters said, "My husband thinks I sew as well as his sisters," and "I'm rereading my copy of Ovid in Latin. It's not bad!" and "Winter is sooo long this year, I hate it. Osman has already taught me all he knows about the stars." No one could make sense of who she was now or put the parts together. There were no children and no pregnancies that anyone heard about, and the family avoided asking.

Her brother was finally about to get himself over for a visit, when Kiki wrote to say, "Guess what? I'm coming back at last. For good. Cannot wait to see you all."

"Cannot wait, my ass," her brother said. "She waited fine. What's so irresistible now?"

No, the husband was not coming with her. "My life here has reached its natural conclusion," Kiki wrote. "Osman will be my dear friend forever but we've come to the end of our road."

"So who ran around on who?" the relatives kept asking. "She'll never say, will she?"

•

Everybody wondered what she would look like when she arrived. Would she be sun-dried and weather-beaten, would she wear billowing silk trousers like a belly dancer, would the newer buildings of New York amaze her, would she gape at the Twin Towers? None of the above. She looked like the same old Kiki, thirty-one with very good skin, and she was wearing jeans and a turtleneck, possibly the same ones she'd left home with. She said, "God! Look at YOU!" when she saw her brother, grown from a scrawny teenager to a man in a sport jacket. She said, "Been a while, hasn't it?" to her dad.

Her luggage was a mess, very third-world, woven plastic valises baled up with string, and there were a lot of them. She had brought back nine carpets! What was she thinking? She wanted to sell them. To someone or other.

Her brother always remembered that when they ate their first meal together, Kiki held her knife and fork like a European. She laughed at things lightly, as if the absurdity of it all wasn't worth shrieking over. She teased Alan about his eyeglasses ("you look like a genius in them") and his large appetite ("has not changed since you were eight"). She certainly sounded like herself. Wasn't she tired from her flight? "No big deal," she said.

She'd had a crappy job in a bookstore before going off on her travels, so what was she going to do now? Did she have any friends left from before? It seemed that she did. Before very long, she moved in with someone named Marcy she'd known at Brooklyn College. Marcy's mother bought the biggest of the rugs, and Kiki used the proceeds to start renting a storefront in the East Village, where she displayed her carpets and other items she had brought back—a brass tea set and turquoise beads and cotton pants with gathered hems that she herself had once worn.

The store stayed afloat for a while. Her brother sort of wondered if she was dealing drugs—hashish was all over Istanbul in the movie *Midnight Express*, which came out just before her return. Kiki refused to see such a film, with its lurid scenes of mean Turkish prisons. "Who has *nice* prisons?" she said. "Name me one single country in the world. Just one."

When her store began to fail and she had to give it up, Kiki supported herself by cleaning houses. She evidently did this with a good spirit; the family was much more embarrassed about it than she was. "People here don't know *how* to clean their houses," she would say. "It's sort of remarkable, isn't it?"

By the time I was a little kid, Kiki had become the assistant director of a small agency that booked housekeepers and nannies. She was the one you got on the phone, the one who didn't take any nonsense from either clients or workers. She was friendly but strict and kept people on point.

I was only a teeny bit afraid of her as a child. She could be very withering if I was acting up and getting crazy and knocking over chairs. But when my parents took me to visit, Kiki had special cookies for me (I loved Mallomars), and for a while she had a boyfriend named Hernando who would play airplane with me and go buzzing around the room. I loved visiting her.

My father told me later that Hernando had wanted to marry Kiki. "But she wasn't made for marriage," he said. "It's not all roses, you know." He and my mother had a history of having, as they say, their differences.

"Kiki was always like a bird," my father said. "Flying here and there."

What a corny thing to say.

I grew up on the outskirts of Boston, in a neighborhood whose leafy familiarity I spurned once I was old enough for hip disdain. I moved to New York as soon as I finished high school, which I barely did. My parents and I were not on good terms in my early years in the city. They hated the guy I first took off with, and my defense of him often turned into insulting them. And I really had no use for more school, and they could never take this in. But Kiki made a point of keeping in touch. She'd call on the phone and say, "I'm thirsty, let's go have a drink. Okay?" At first I was up in Inwood, as far north in Manhattan as you can get, so it was a long subway ride to see her in the East Village, but once I moved to Harlem it wasn't quite so bad. When my son was born, four years ago, Kiki brought me the most useful layette of baby stuff, things a person couldn't even know she needed. Oliver would calm down and sleep when she walked him around. He grew up calling her Aunt Great Kiki.

The two of us lived in a housing project, one of the nicer ones, in an apartment illegally passed on to me by a boyfriend. It was a decent size, with good light, and I liked my neighbors. They were a great mix, and nobody wanted to rat on me about the lease. They'd stopped thinking I was another white gentrifier, sneaking in.

In late October of the year that the TV kept telling us to get prepared for Hurricane Sandy, Oliver had a great time flicking the flashlight on and off (a really annoying game) and watching me tape giant x's on the window glass. All the kids on our hallway were hyped up and excited, running around and yelling. We kept looking out the windows as the sky turned a sepia tint. When the rains broke and began to come down hard, we could hear the moaning of the winds and everything clattering and banging in the night, awnings and trees getting the hell beaten out of them. I kept switching to different channels on TV so we wouldn't miss any of it. The television had better coverage than my view out the window. Through the screen a newscaster in a suit told us the Con Ed substation on Fourteenth Street had exploded! The lights in the bottom of Manhattan had gone out! I made efforts to explain to Oliver about electricity, as if I knew. Never, never put your finger in a socket. Oliver wanted to watch a better program.

At nine thirty the phone rang and it was my father, who had more patience with me these days but didn't call that often. He was calling to say, "Your aunt Kiki doesn't have power, you know. She's probably sitting in the dark." I had forgotten about her entirely. She was on East Fifth Street, in the no-electricity zone. I promised I'd check on Kiki in the morning.

"I might have to walk there," I said. "It's like a hundred twenty blocks. You're not going to ask about my neighborhood? It's fine."

"How's Oliver?"

"Great."

"Don't forget about Kiki, okay? Tell me that."

"I just told you," I said.

The weather outside was shockingly pleasant the next day, mild with a white sky. We walked for half an hour, which Oliver really did not like, past some downed trees and tossed branches, and then a cab miraculously stopped and we shared it with an old guy all the way downtown. No traffic lights, no stores open—how strange the streets were. In Kiki's building, I led Oliver up four flights of dark tenement stairs while he drove me nuts flicking the flashlight on and off.

When Kiki opened the door onto her pitch-black hallway, she said, "Reyna! What are you doing here?"

Kiki, of course, was fine. She had plenty of vegetables and canned food and rice—who needed a fridge?—and she could light the stove with a match. She had daylight now and candles for later. She had pots of water she could boil to wash with. The tub had been filled the night before. How was I? "Oliver, isn't this fun?" she said.

Oh, New Yorkers were making such a big fuss, she

thought. She had a transistor radio so the fussing came through. "I myself am enjoying the day off from work," she said. She was rereading *The Greek Way* by Edith Hamilton—had I ever read it? I didn't read much, did I?— and she planned to finish it tonight by candlelight.

"Come stay with us," I said. "Wouldn't you like that, Oliver?"

Oliver crowed on cue.

Kiki said she always preferred being in her own home. "Oliver, I bet you would like some of the chocolate ice cream that's turning into a lovely milkshake."

We followed her into the kitchen, with its painted cabinets and old linoleum. When I took off my jacket to settle in, Kiki said, "Oh, no. Did you get a new tattoo?"

"No. You always say that. You're phobic about my arms."

"I'll never get used to them."

I had a dove and a sparrow and a tiger lily and a branch with leaves. They all stood for things. The dove was to settle a fight with Oliver's father, who was much less nice than Boyd, my current boyfriend; the sparrow was the true New York bird; the tiger lily meant boldness, which I was big on when I was younger; and the branch was an olive tree in honor of Oliver. I used to try to tell Kiki they were no different from the patterns on rugs. "Are you a floor?" she said. She accused my tattoos of being forms of mutilation and also forms of deception against my natural skin. According to what? "Well, Islamic teaching, for one thing," she said.

Kiki had never been a practicing Muslim but she liked a lot of it. I may have been the only one in the family who knew how into it she'd once been. She used to try to get me to read this unreadable guy Averroes and also another one, Avicenna. Only my aunt would think someone like me could just dip into twelfth-century philosophy if I felt like it. She saw no reason why not.

"Oliver, my boy," she was saying now, "you don't have to finish if you're full."

"Dad's worried about you," I told Kiki.

"I already called him," she said. It turned out her phone still worked because she had an old landline, nothing digital or bundled.

She'd been outside earlier in the day. Some people on her block had water but she didn't. Oliver was entranced when Kiki showed him how she flushed the toilet by throwing down a potful of water.

"It's magic," I said.

When we left, Kiki called after us, "I'm always glad to see you, you know that." She could have given us more credit for getting all the way there, I thought.

"You might change your mind about staying with us," I called back, before we went out into the dark hallway.

I had an extra reason for wanting her to stay. Not to be one of those mothers who was always desperate for baby-sitting, but I needed a babysitter.

My boyfriend was spending three months at Rikers Island. For all of October I'd gone to see him once a week. He was there for selling five ounces of weed (who thinks

that should even be a crime?) and it made a big difference to him to have someone visit. I planned to go there
again this week, once the subways were back on and buses
were going over the bridge again. But it was hard bringing
Oliver, who wasn't his kid and who needed a lot of attention during those toyless visits.

I loved Boyd but I wouldn't have said I loved him more
than the others I'd been with. Fortunately no one asked.
Not even Boyd. There was no need for people to keep
mouthing off about how much they felt, in his view. Some
degree of real interest, some persistence in showing up,
was enough. Every week I watched him waiting in that visitors' room, another young African American in a stupid
jumpsuit. The sight of him—heavy-faced, wary, waiting to
smile slightly—always got to me, and when I hugged him
(light hugs were permitted), I'd think, *It's still Boyd, it's
Boyd here.*

Oliver could be a nuisance. Sometimes he was very,
very whiney from standing in too many different lines, or
he was incensed that he couldn't bring in his giant plastic
dinosaur. Or he got overstimulated and had to nestle up to
Boyd and complain at length about some kid who threw
sand in the park. "You having adventures, right?" Boyd
said. Meanwhile, I was trying to ask Boyd if he'd had an
okay week and why not. I had an hour to give him the joys
of my conversation. Dealing with those two at once was
not the easiest.

•

I got a phone call from Aunt Kiki on the second day after the hurricane. "How would you feel about my coming over after work to take a hot shower?" she said. "I can bring a towel, I've got piles of towels."

"Our shower is dying to see you," I said. "And Oliver will lend you his ducky."

"Kiki Kiki Kiki Kiki Kiki!" Oliver yelled, when she came through the door. Maybe I'd worked him up too much in advance. We'd gotten the place very clean.

When my aunt came out of the bathroom, dressed again in her slacks and sweater and with a steamed-pink face under the turban of her towel, I handed her a glass of red wine. "A person without heat or water needs alcohol," I said. And we sat down to meat loaf, which I was good at, and mashed potatoes, which Oliver had learned to eat with garlic.

"This is a feast," she said. "Did you know the sultans had feasts that went on for two weeks?"

Oliver was impressed. "This one could go on longer," I said. "You should stay over. Or come back tomorrow. I mean it."

Tomorrow was what I needed—it was the visiting night for inmates with last names from M to Z.

"Maybe the power will be back by then," Kiki said. "Maybe maybe."

At Rikers, Boyd and the others had spent the hurricane under lockdown, no wandering off into the torrent. Rikers had its own generator, and the buildings were in the center of the island, too high to wash away. It was never meant to be a place you might swim from.

"You know I have this boyfriend, Boyd," I said.

Kiki was looking at her plate while I gave her the situation, about the weekly visits, as much as I could tell in front of Oliver. "Oh, shit," she said. She had to finish chewing to say, "Okay, sure, okay, I'll come right from work."

When I leaned over to embrace her, she seemed embarrassed. "Oh, please," she said. "No big deal."

What an interesting person Kiki was. What could I ever say to her that would throw her for a loop? Best not to push it, of course. No need to warn her not to tell my parents either. Not Kiki. And maybe she had a boyfriend of her own that I didn't even know about. She wasn't someone who told you everything. She wasn't showering with him, wherever he was. Maybe he was married. A man that age. Oh, where was I going with this?

When Kiki turned up the next night, she was forty-five minutes later than she'd said, and I had given up on her several times over. She bustled through the door saying, "Don't ask me how the subways are running. Go, go. Get out of here, go."

She looked younger, all flushed like that. What a babe she must've once been. Or at least a hippie sweetheart. Oliver clambered all over her. "Will you hurry up and get out of here?" she said to me.

•

The subway (which had only started running that day) was indeed slow to arrive and very crowded, but the bus near Queens Plaza that went to Rikers was the same as ever. After the first few stops, all the white people emptied out except for me. I read *People* magazine while we inched our way toward the bridge to the island; love was making a mess of the lives of any number of celebrities. And look at that teenage girl across the aisle in the bus, combing her hair, checking it in a mirror, pulling the strands across her face to make it hang right. *Girl*, I wanted to say, *he fucked up bad enough to get himself where he is, and you're still worried he won't like your hair?*

Of course, I was all moussed and lipsticked myself. I had standards. But you couldn't wear anything too re-vealing—no rips or see-through—they had rules. *Visitors must wear undergarments.*

Poor Boyd. After I stood in a line and put my coat and purse in a locker and showed my ID to the guards and got searched and stood in a line for one of Rikers's own buses and got searched again, I sat in the room to wait for him. It was odd being there without Oliver. The wait went on too long. It wasn't like you could bring a book to occupy you. And then I heard Boyd's familiar name, read from the list.

Those jumpsuits didn't flatter anyone. But when we hugged, he smelled of soap and Boyd, and I was sorry for myself to have him away so long. "Hey, there," he said.

"Didn't mean to get here so late," I said.

Boyd wanted to hear about the hurricane and who got

hit the worst. Aunt Kiki became my material. "Oh, she had her candles and her pots of water and her cans of soup and her bags of rice, she couldn't see why everybody was so upset."

"Can't keep 'em down, old people like that," he said. "Good for her. That's the best thing I've heard all week."

I went on about the gameness of Kiki. The way she'd taught me the right way to climb trees when I was young, when my mother was only worried I'd fall on my head.

"I didn't know you were a climber. Have to tell Claude."

His friend Claude, much more of an athlete than Boyd was, had recently discovered the climbing wall at some gym. Boyd himself was a couch potato, but a lean and lanky one. Was he getting puffy now? A little.

"Claude's a monster on that wall. Got Lynnette doing it too." Lynnette was Claude's sister. And Boyd's last girl-friend before me. "Girls can do that stuff fine, he says."

"When did he say that?"

"They came by last week. The whole gang."

What gang? Only three visitors allowed. "Lynnette was here?"

"And Maxwell. They came to show support. I appreci-ated it, you know?"

I'll bet you did, I thought. I was trying not to leap to any conclusions. It wasn't as if she could've crept into the corner with him for a quickie, though you heard rumors of such things. Urban myths.

"Does Claude still have that stringy haircut?"

"He does. Looks like a root vegetable. Man should go

to my barber." The Rikers barber had given Boyd an onion look, if you were citing vegetables.

"They're coming again Saturday. You're not coming Saturday, right?"

I never came on Saturdays. I cut him a look.

"Because if you are," he said, "I'll tell them not to come."

You couldn't blame a man who had nothing for wanting everything he could get his hands on. This was pretty much what I thought on the bus ride back to the subway. Oh, I could blame him. I was spending an hour and a half to get there every week and an hour and a half to get home, so he could entertain his ex? I was torn between being pissed off and my preference for not making trouble. But why had Boyd told me? The guy could keep his mouth shut when he needed to.

He didn't think he needed to. Because I was a good sport. What surprised me even more was how painful this was starting to be. I could imagine Boyd greeting Lynnette, in his offhand, Mr. Cool way. "Can't believe you dropped in." Lynnette silky and tough, telling him it had been too long. But what was so great about Boyd that I should twist in torment from what I was seeing too clearly in my head?

I was sitting on the bus during this anguish. I wanted Boyd to comfort me. He had a talent for that. If you were insulted because some asshole at daycare said your kid's shoes were unsuitable, if you splurged on a nice TV and then realized you'd overpaid, if you got fired from your job because you used up sick days and it wasn't your fault, Boyd could make it seem hilarious. He could imitate people he'd never met. He could remind you it was part of the ever-expanding joke of human trouble. Not just you.

When I got back to the apartment, Oliver was actually asleep in his bed—had Kiki drugged him?—and Kiki was in the living room watching the Cooking Channel on TV. "You watch this crap?" I said.

"How was the visit?"

"Medium. Who's winning on *Chopped*?"

"The wrong guy. But I have a thing for Marcus Samuelsson." He was the judge who had a restaurant right here in Harlem, a chef born in Ethiopia, tall and good-looking. Good for Kiki.

"Oliver spilled a lot of yogurt on the floor but we got it cleaned up," she said.

I wanted a drink, I wanted a joint. What was in the house? I found a very used bottle of Beaujolais in the kitchen and poured glasses for us both.

"When does he get out?" Kiki asked.

"They say January. He's holding up okay."

"He has you."

So he did. I'd gotten more attached to Boyd, from all my visiting in that place, from our weekly private talking in that big public room. We made our own little kingdom of conversation, however awkward it was, the two of us saying whatever came to us, with the chairs and the tables around us the sites of other families' dramas. We had our snacks from the machine and our stories; the two of us and Oliver. Sometimes Oliver got us silly; it was all very precious. And every week I admired the way Boyd hosted us, the way he settled into the plastic chair as if we were just hanging out, waiting, on our way to some place better. Which we were.

"You don't have to tell me if you don't want to, but when you got divorced," I said to Kiki, "was it because one of you had been messing around with someone else?"

"Hey," Kiki said, "where did that come from?"

"Someone named Lynnette has been visiting Boyd."

Kiki considered this. "Could be nothing."

"So when you left Turkey, why did you leave?"

"It was time."

I admired Kiki's way of deciding what was none of your business, but it made you think there was business there.

And it was my bad luck that Con Ed got its act together the very next evening, so electricity flowed in the walls of Kiki's home to give her light and refrigeration and to pump her water and the gurgling steam in her radiators. I called her to say Happy Normal.

"Normal is overrated," she said. "I'll be so busy next week."

"Me, too," I said.

Oliver hardly ever had sitters. He was in daycare while

I went off to my unglamorous employment as a part-time receptionist at a veterinarian's office (it paid lousy but the dogs were usually nice), and at night I took him with me if I went to friends' or to Boyd's, when I used to stay with Boyd. Sometimes Boyd had a cousin who took him.

"Oliver wants to say hi," I told my aunt.

"I *love* you, Great Kiki!" Oliver said.

This didn't move her to volunteer to sit for him again, and I thought it was better not to ask again so soon.

Oliver wasn't bad at all on the next visit to Rikers. And one of the guards at the first gate was nicely jokey with him. Because he was a kid? Because he was a white kid with a white mother? I didn't know but I was glad.

The weather was colder outside and he got to wear his favorite Spiderman sweater, which Boyd said was very sharp.

"Your mom's looking good too," Boyd said.

"Better than Lynnette?"

I hadn't meant to say any such whiny-bitch thing, it leaped out of me. I was horrified. I wasn't as good as I thought I was, was I?

"Not in your league," Boyd said. "Girl's nowhere near." He said this slowly and soberly. He shook his onion head for emphasis.

And the rest of the visit went very well. Boyd suggested that Oliver now had superpowers to spin webs from the ceiling—"You going to float above us all, land right on all the bad guys"—and Oliver was so tickled he had to be stopped from shrieking with glee at top volume.

"Know what I miss?" Boyd said. "Well, that, of course. Don't look at me that way. But also I miss when we used to go ice-skating."

We had gone exactly twice, renting skates in Central Park, falling on our asses. I almost crushed Oliver one time I went down. "You telling everyone you're the next big hockey star?" I said.

"I hope there's still ice when I get out," he said.

"There will be," I said. "It's soon. Before you know it."

Kiki had now started to worry about me; she called more often than I was used to. She'd say, "You think Obama's going to get this Congress in line? And how's Boyd doing?"

I let her know we were still an item, which was what she wanted to know. Why in God's name would I ever think of splitting up with Boyd before I could at least get him back home and in bed again? What was the point of all these bus rides if I was going to skip that part?

"You wouldn't want me to desert him at a time like this," I said.

"Be careful," she said.

"He's not much of a criminal," I said. "He was just a bartender, not any big-time guy." I didn't have to tell her not to mention this to my father.

"Anybody can be in jail, I know that," Kiki said. "Hikmet was in jail for thirteen years in Turkey."

I thought she meant an old flame of hers but it turned out she meant a famous poet, who was dead before she even got there. A famous Communist poet. One of the prisons he'd been in was near where she went in her years there and people had pointed it out. Nice to hear she was open-minded on the jail question. Kiki had views beyond most white people.

Boyd wasn't in jail for politics, although some people claimed the war on drugs was a race war, and they had a point. My mom and dad were known to smoke dope every now and then, and was any cop stop-and-frisking them on the streets of their nice neighborhood?

"So can I ask you," I said, "were there drugs around when you were in Turkey?" What a blurter I was these days. "Were people selling hash or anything?"

"Not in our circles. I hate that movie, you've seen that movie. But there was smuggling. I mean in antiquities, bits from ancient sites. People went across to the eastern parts, brought stuff back. Or they got it over the border from Iran. Beautiful things, really."

"It's amazing what people get money for."

"If Osman had wanted to do that," she said, "he wouldn't have become a farmer. It was the farming that made me leave, by the way."

I was very pleased that she told me.

"And he left off farming five years later," she said. "Wasn't that ironic?"

"It was," I said.

"I still write to Osman. He's a great letter-writer."

This was news. Did she have all the letters, how hot were they, did he email now? Of course, I was thinking: *Maybe you two should get back together.* It's a human impulse, isn't it, to want to set the world in couples.

"The wife he has now is much younger," Kiki said.

By December I'd gotten a new tattoo in honor of Boyd's impending release from Rikers. It was quite beautiful—a birdcage with the door open and a whole line of tiny birds going up toward my wrist. Some people designed their body art so it all fit together, but I did mine piecemeal, like my life, and it looked fine.

Kiki noticed it when it was a week old and still swollen. She had just made supper for us (overcooked hamburgers but Oliver liked them) and I was doing the dishes, keeping that arm out of the water. Soaking too soon was bad for it.

"And when Boyd is out of the picture," Kiki said, "you'll be stuck with this ink that won't go away."

"It's my history," I said. "My arm is an album." I got my first tattoo when I was sixteen, the tiger lily, when I ran away with a boyfriend who made off with his father's truck to take us to a chilly beach in Maine for a week. I loved that tattoo. And the olive branch for Oliver had been done a month after his birth, when I wanted to remind myself to be happy.

"What if Boyd doesn't like this one?"

"It's for *me*," I said. "All of these are *mine*."

"Don't be a carpet," she said.

"You don't really know very much about this," I said, "if you don't mind my saying."

Why would I take advice from a woman who slept every night alone in her bed, cuddling up with some copy of Aristotle? What could she possibly tell me that I could use? And she was getting older by the minute, with her squinty eyes and her short hair stuck too close to her head.

It was snowing the day Boyd got released from Rikers. I was home with Oliver when his friend Maxwell went to pick him up. He didn't want me and Oliver seeing him then, with his bag of items, with his humbling paperwork, with the guards leaning over every detail. By the time I got to view Boyd he was in our local coffee shop with Maxwell, eating a cheeseburger, looking happy and greasy. Oliver went berserk, leaping all over him, smearing his little snowy boots all over Boyd's pants. I leaped a little too. "Don't knock me over," Boyd said. "Nah, knock me over. Go ahead."

"Show him no mercy," Maxwell said.

Already Boyd looked vastly better than he had in jail, and he'd only been out an hour. "Can't believe it," he said. "Can't believe I was ever there." He fed French fries to Oliver, who pretended to be a dog. Boyd had his other hand on my knee. We could do that now. "Hey, girl," he said. The snow outside the window gave everything a lunar brightness.

•

The first night he stayed with me, after it took forever to get Oliver asleep in the other room, I was madly eager when we made our way to each other at last. How did it go, this dream, did we still know how to do this? We knew just fine, we knew all along, but there were fumbles and pauses, little laughing hesitations. I had imagined Boyd would be hungry and even rough, but, no, he was careful, careful; he looped around and circled back and took some sweet byways before settling on his goal. He was trying, it seemed to me, to make this first contact very particular, trying to recognize me. I didn't expect this from him, which showed what I knew.

At my job in the vet's office my fellow workers teased me about being sleepy at the desk. They all knew my boyfriend had returned after a long trip. Any yawn brought on group hilarity. "Look how she walks, she hobbles," one of the techs said. What a raunchy office I worked in, people who dealt with animals. All I said was, "Laugh away, you're green with envy."

I was distracted, full of wayward thoughts—Boyd and I starting a restaurant together, Boyd and I running off to Thailand, Boyd and I having a kid together, maybe a girl, what would we name her, Oliver would like this, or would he? I lost focus while I was doing my tasks at the computer and had to put up with everyone saying how sleepy I was.

•

Jail doesn't always change people in good ways, but in Boyd's case it made him quieter and less apt to throw his weight around. He had to find a new job (no alcohol), which was a big challenge to his stylish self. I was sort of proud of him when he started in as a waiter in a diner just north of our neighborhood. This was definitely a step down for him, which he bore grudgingly but not bitterly. His hair at night smelled of frying oil and broiler smoke. His home was not exactly with me—he was officially camped out at his cousin's, since his own apartment was gone—but he spent a lot of nights at my place. I liked the cousin (Maxwell, who had sometimes babysat for Oliver), but he had a tendency to drag Boyd out to clubs at night. In my younger days I liked to go clubbing same as anyone but once I had Oliver it pretty much lost its appeal. I had reason to imagine girls in little itty-bitty outfits were busy throwing themselves at Boyd in these clubs, but it turned out that wasn't the problem. The problem was that Maxwell had a scheme for increasing Boyd's admittedly paltry income. It had to do with smuggling cigarettes from Virginia to New York, of all idiotic ways to make a profit. Just to cash in on the tax difference. "Are you out of your fucking mind?" I said. "You want to violate probation?"

"Don't shout," Boyd said.

"Crossing state lines. Are you crazy?"

"That's it," Boyd said. "You always have opinions. Topic closed. Forget I said a word."

I didn't take well to being shushed. I snapped at him and he got stony and went home early that night. "A man needs peace, is that too much to ask?" When would he be back? Did I give a fuck?

"You think I give a fuck?" I said.

I was with Kiki the next day, having lunch near my office. She was checking up on me these days as much as she could, which included treating me to the mixed falafel plate. I told her about the dog I'd met at my job who knew three languages. It could sit, lie down, and beg in English, Spanish, and ASL. "A pit bull mix. They're very smart."

"You know what I think?" Kiki said. "I think you should go live somewhere where you'd learn another language. Everyone should really."

"Someday," I said.

"I still have a friend in Istanbul. I bet you and Oliver could go camp out at her place. For a little while. It's a very kid-friendly culture."

"I don't think so. My life is here."

"It doesn't have to be Istanbul, that was my place, it's not everyone's. There are other places. I'd stake you with some cash if you wanted to take off for a while."

I wasn't even tempted.

"It's very good of you," I said.

"You'll be sorry later if you don't do it," she said.

She wanted to get me away from Boyd, which might happen on its own anyway. I was touched and insulted, both at once. And then I was trying to imagine myself in a new city. Taking Oliver to a park in Rome. Having interesting chats with the locals while I sat on the bench. Laughing away in Italian.

My phone interrupted us with the ping sound that meant I was getting a text. "Sorry," I said to Kiki. "I just need to check." It was Boyd, and I was so excited that I said, "Oh! From Boyd!" out loud. *Sorry, Baby* was in the message, and some extra parts that I certainly wasn't reading to Kiki. But I chuckled in joy, tickled to death—I could feel myself getting flushed. How funny he could be when he wanted. That Boyd.

"Excuse me," I said. "I just have to answer fast."

"Go ahead," Kiki said, not pleasantly.

I had to concentrate to tap the letters. It took a few minutes, and I could hear Kiki sigh across from me. I knew how I looked, too girly, too jacked up over crumbs Boyd threw my way. Kiki was not glad about it. She didn't even know Boyd. But I did—I could see him very distinctly in my mind just then, his grumbling sweetness, his spells of cold scorn, his sad illusions about what he could do, and the waves of tenderness I had for him, the sudden pangs of adoration. I was perfectly aware (or just then I was, anyway) that some part of my life with Boyd was not entirely real, that if you pushed it too hard a whole other feeling would show itself. I wasn't about to push. I wanted us to go on as we were. A person can know several things at once. I could know all of them while still being moved to delight by him—his kisses on my neck, his way of humming to the most blaring tune, his goofing around with Oliver. And then I saw that I was probably going to help him with the cigarette smuggling too. I was going to be in it with him before I even meant to be.

If Kiki knew, she'd wail in despair. I was going to pack the car and count out the cash; I was going to let him store his illegal cigarettes in my house. All because of what stirred me, all because of what Boyd was to me. All because of beauty.

I had my own life to live. And what did Kiki have? She had her job making deals between the very rich and the very poor. She had her books that she settled inside of in dusty private satisfaction. She had her old and fabled past. I loved my aunt, but she must have known I'd never listen to her.

When I stopped texting Boyd, I looked up, and Kiki was dabbing at her plate of food. "The hummus was good," I said.

"They say Saladin ate hummus," she said. "In the 1100s. You know him, right? He was a Kurd who fought against the Crusaders."

She knew a lot. She was waiting for me to make some fucking effort to know a fraction as much. Saladin who? In the meantime—anyone looking at our table could've seen this—we were having a long and unavoidable moment, my aunt and I, of each feeling sorry for the other. In our separate ways. How could we not?

2

In all those three months that Boyd was away at Rikers, certain images of him kept me company. The sexy parts. Well, of course. Who wouldn't hold on to those? The way he raised his arm to reach for me in bed, the transformed look on his face when his eyes were closed, a grunt of praise in his throat for something I was doing. So when the actual Boyd returned, real life confused me at first. It was less abstract and it had more speech in it. I had all that longing and then I had this person to talk to.

What did we talk about? Whether Oliver was out of line when he threw his dinosaur at me, whether Rihanna had a better voice than Beyoncé ever did, why people in restaurants could never fucking order logically.

Boyd was not happy in his work at the diner. But didn't a man who'd tended bar have ways to maneuver people so they knew better than to give him a hard time? He did. He had to display just enough personality as a waiter to throw a healthy fear into patrons. The thing I wanted least was for Boyd to walk out on this job. His probation officer and I were of one mind on that topic.

And I was hoping the new cigarette-smuggling scheme was just talk. "Hey," I said, "you don't even *smoke* cigarettes anymore." He'd gone to the trouble of quitting in the last year, and what a cosmic pain that was. He was moody and hostile, and after a month he lapsed and smoked himself into a stupor for another few months before he quit again. He did too many nicotine patches; he almost ruined his teeth sucking hard candy and chewing gummy bears for distraction. And now he wanted to go all the way to fucking Virginia just to load a car with Marlboros.

The one thing I had to be careful not to do was speak against his cousin Maxwell. Boyd could cut me dead with a look if I said as much as, "Maxwell has too many ideas."

At breakfast one morning, Oliver told a long story about his friend Hector at daycare playing a trick on him and running off with a truck they were playing with. Boyd said, "I think this Hector dude is not your friend. Friends don't act sneaky. Don't you be sneaky, be loyal, you hear what I'm saying?"

I thought this was a bit much for a four-year-old but Oliver nodded sagely.

By the end of the first two weeks Boyd was better about the diner. He was telling me stories about the great ketchup wars, where a single bottle got grabbed by different tables, so he had to toss and catch it behind his back to chill everybody out. He gave all the customers nicknames—"got to keep things interesting"—and they liked that, they wanted to be his.

Maxwell's apartment was the housing approved for Boyd by the probation board. I didn't get the sense anyone was checking all that carefully, but Boyd liked to refer to his stays with me as "slipping away." This was a sexy way to put it. One night he called me at midnight from Maxwell's—he woke me up—and I could hear the guys talking and goofing in the background. "Whole group going out, but you know I want to go to you," he said. "What do you think?"

I knew what I thought. I could sleep when I was ninety. And the sound of his key in the door some twenty minutes later was an erotic noise, the clicking and the turning in the lock. I was in the hallway right away, with my finger to my lips, but he knew to be quiet, not to get Oliver up. We walked into the bedroom like cat burglars, and he shut the door with perfect slowness, my stealth lover.

We faced each other in a great clasping hug—I'd overheard Boyd telling Claude how "tight" we were these days, and the metaphor of this was in the force of that grasp, the long grip of it. We held on for a while. Then Boyd backed me onto the bed—he could be very adroit—and he hardly had to unwrap himself to somehow get out of his clothes.

The whole time I was making my weekly visits to Rikers, being the good girlfriend, I only thought about his getting out of there soon. That was enough to look forward to then. I never guessed we'd be in anything like a new phase once he was out, and I didn't ever think at all that a spirit so much like happiness would be involved.

When I got up from bed the next morning, to get Oliver fed and off to daycare, Boyd was lying with his arm thrown across his face, dead asleep and faraway. But once Oliver was awake, my son went into noisy-boy mode and started squealing about which socks he hated, and by the time I went back to check, Boyd was sitting up in bed, eyes tracking me. "All the guys that went out last night," he said, "just hoping they find someone a hundredth as good as you."

You carry yourself differently when you have a line like that to recall all day. I wasn't above being thrilled to death by good words. Even my friend Sabina, who always said, "Why do we talk about men so much?" snickered in appreciation when I told her. I almost quoted him to Aunt Kiki when I talked to her on the phone, but I had some sense.

"You know what I was just reading again last night?" Kiki said. "Marcus Aurelius."

"I wasn't going to guess that."

"You'd love him. He's all about being calm, guarding your mind. You should read him, the Stoics are good."

Boyd liked to say one thing I was really good at was keeping calm.

"I'm so cool I don't need him," I said. "The man could learn from me." Except that he was dead, which always inhibited learning.

"The thing about the Stoics," Kiki said, "they're like hyper-rational Buddhists. Seneca said we're all dying every day. Epictetus said we're all little souls carrying around our corpses."

"Is something not all right?" I said.

"No problem," she said. "Everything's fine."

Meanwhile, Boyd was so much at ease these days that on the Monday we wanted to go ice-skating but couldn't because it was already too warm, he took Oliver and me to hang out at the café in Brooklyn where my friend Sabina worked, and we had a Williamsburg afternoon, which was not his thing at all. But he was cool with everything—panini with almost nothing to eat between the bread, Sabina whining about having no money, white guys with hair combed forward like Napoleon (I hated that haircut), Oliver running around like a little maniac.

I thanked Boyd for his patience when we got home. "Hey, don't worry," he said.

It was only when I left Oliver at my neighbor's one night and I joined the crew at Maxwell's—a bunch of guys and a few girls around the edges—that I got a feel for what was improving Boyd's attitude. Anyone could see he was much more with it now, and it was the promise of criminal glory that was giving him his style back. I should've known;

maybe I had known. They were all talking about getting some vehicle to go to Virginia with. Could they get hold of a truck, did they need a van, what about a car with a big trunk? Could they borrow a car from anybody?

I didn't say to Boyd, "Well, you can't even fucking drive," since he was touchy about remarks in front of his friends. Everyone knew his license was suspended for six months (they did that to drug offenders, even minor ones like him) and he wasn't supposed to go out of state either, unless he had special approval. The man had every reason to stay put.

Lots of New Yorkers never learned how to drive. It turned out Maxwell, Mr. Mastermind, was one of them. Claude said, "I can do it, you know."

Lynnette, his sister—and why was she here?—said, "You're the worst driver in the world, ask the whole neighborhood."

"Like you're any better," he said.

They weren't going to get this together. It didn't strike me as a serious discussion, with everyone and his girlfriend putting in their two cents. In my own opinion, which I did utter aloud, just because the same pack of cigarettes had a $0.30 tax in Virginia and a $5.85 tax in New York City (kind of amazing) didn't mean any of them should get anywhere near this idea.

"And you really think a bunch of guys like you with New York plates are going to be invisible to cops on the highways of Virginia?" I said.

"No law against driving," Claude said.

"You ever drive a truck?" Maxwell said to me.

In fact, I had. In high school I had a beloved boyfriend whose father was a contractor, the one I ran away to Maine with, and we both liked the goofiness of me behind the wheel. I should've kept this fact to myself, but what I said was, "Of course."

This made them laugh. They were looking at Boyd, who'd brought me into this. I'd stuck by him when lots of girls never bothered making the long trek to Rikers. I wasn't the only white person in the room either (Maxwell's friend Wiley was with a pretty Dominican, a mix of everything, and there was a blond guy from the Bronx who was somebody's buddy). They were used to me, all of them, for better and worse. Lynnette never liked me, but I didn't think her reasons were racial.

And then somebody wanted to know how much gas cost in Virginia, and didn't a truck have the worst mpg of anything you could think of? Claude got all caught up in checking statistics on his smartphone. None of them knew about cars.

Lynnette said, "Wait a few months and then Boyd can do it. He'll be fine."

Boyd gave one of his slow smiles. Well, anyone liked praise.

I called my parents to ask if they had any clue what was up with Kiki. She wasn't old—sixties weren't old nowadays— why was she talking about death?

"Kiki doesn't tell me anything," my father said. "But she gets like this before she sees her friend Pat. They've known each other so long. *Tempus fugit*, she's thinking."

Pat was her old best friend from Turkey, and every summer they went off to Cape Cod together to hang out at the beach. They'd been doing this for thirty years.

"I bet they just talk about their ex-husbands," my mother said. "Obsolete gossip. How's Oliver? You never tell us how Oliver is."

"Kiki's healthy, right?"

"You always worry about her," my mother said. "Do you worry about us?"

Oliver had started asking me if I could get him a brother. "Older or younger?"

"Both!" he said. His friend Hector at daycare had a big messy family Oliver wanted.

"Not the worst idea," Boyd said, and he put his hand on my hip.

I practically teared up, I was that touched and surprised. Except that it actually was the worst idea.

"*I* don't have a brother or sister," I said to Oliver. "Boyd has a brother in the army he never sees."

"Don't just give him the negative," Boyd said. "Look at Claude and Lynnette."

Lynnette would never be my favorite, but it was true she went ballistic at anyone who spoke a word against her brother, and when Claude got arrested for shoplifting a coat, it was Lynnette who went to the police station, Lynnette who took care of it. When Lynnette got fired from a job, when Lynnette burned through all her credit, it was Claude who kept her fed. They bickered when they were together—Claude said, "Shut it, girl," and Lynnette said, "What a dick you can be"—but this was their coziness.

Oliver said, "I never get anything I want."

In April, Maxwell started talking about how somebody's brother-in-law would sell them his old Ford Taurus for a good price. Did we know how big the trunks were on those dopey little machines? Bigger than you'd think. They just needed investors to chip in for the car. Who had savings? Did I have savings?

"If you're partners with us," Maxwell said to me, "we share the profits. I know you're doing okay with the dogs and cats, but a person can see you could use a little more cash. You got Oliver there."

We were sitting on a bench at the edge of a playground during this discussion. Oliver was climbing up an overdesigned modern jungle gym, and I had an eye on him and the other kids to make sure there was no pushing on the ladder. The guys—Maxwell and Claude and Boyd—had come to visit me where I had to be; they were extending themselves, for guys. As well they might. "Maybe you don't have money," Maxwell said. I did not. "But you could help in other ways. Like if the car is in your name, everything is simpler for us. Just your name, it's nothing."

"I'll think about it," I said. "Okay?"

"Sure," Maxwell said. "No pressure."

Later, at home, when Boyd had his head in my lap while he lay on the sofa watching TV, he said, "You don't have to do anything you don't want to do."

"Then I'd rather not," I said.

The words came out just like that. I hadn't known they were so ready to land. I was a free person, it so happened, and I wasn't afraid of Boyd either.

"I've seen enough of Rikers just visiting," I said. "I'm a mother, you know?"

"It's fine," Boyd said. "No big deal."

He was murmuring into my jeans. I put my hand on his head, and he turned his face to kiss it. Who would think my saying no would have us acting so fond with each other? But we both seemed eager to show we were above financial disputes, we were better than that. He kept his lips against my palm for a good five minutes, while men ran around a green field on TV.

Lynnette didn't mind at all putting her name on the car's registration. They wanted someone with no record (that let out Boyd and Claude), just to keep anything from getting flagged, and Maxwell said it looked too weird for someone like him without a license to own a car. They were paying off the car in installments. For how long?

"It's going to take a minute," Boyd said, which meant a while.

Not the best business model, but maybe that was always how people did these things. I could stay away from most of it. It didn't have to concern me.

"When we drive down in April," Maxwell said, "Virginia's going to look so pretty."

"Do you ever think of going back to Turkey?" I asked my aunt. "Don't you want to see Osman? Don't you wonder what he looks like now?"

"You and Oliver should go there. You could stay with my friend, Pat. You'd like it."

How would Kiki look to her old husband? More than once, I'd imagined meetings with my ex-lovers at later points in life, sometimes on urgent last requests from their sickbeds. And I always appeared when summoned, no matter how shitty they'd once been to me. Why did I conjure this? Of course, I wanted them to beg for me, to be stunned and grateful at the sight of me; I'd show up in tribute to the substance of what we trashed. I always wanted the last triumph of behaving well.

The boys were so happy with their car. It had a few dents and some rust on the bottom and it was a nondescript silver-gray, just right. Claude drove it around the neighborhood (he really was a bad driver, he practically hit a kid), I zoomed up to the Bronx and showed off my fabulous parking skills, and then Maxwell came up with his annoying friend Wiley who was suddenly elected the man behind the wheel for the trip to Virginia. I wasn't a huge fan of Wiley—he had a shifty, sullen act around women—but he'd have Maxwell and Claude with him. Boyd was the one who figured the costs and managed the cash.

They couldn't just walk into some convenience store and buy six hundred cartons of cigarettes. Buying more than twenty-five at a time was illegal now anyway. "We need our very own supplier," Maxwell the capitalist said. Did anyone know a soul in Virginia? Well, Wiley had someone he'd gone to elementary school with, who lived in Richmond now.

I wasn't in on this part, which took a few weeks—lots of phone calls, negotiations I didn't want to hear about. I read online that some officials claimed terrorists and gangs were running cigarettes to finance their evil enterprises. If this was true, then the boys were in for some very serious competition.

"Nobody cares, we're too little an operation," Boyd said.

I showed him on my phone a newspaper article I'd dredged up in my search—"Cigarette Smuggling Linked to Terrorism." A few guys from Lebanon had gone to jail for "funneling" money to Hezbollah from the vast profits of very "lucrative" cigarette smuggling.

"Fuck, I guess you're not making it up," he said. "Not good. But, wait a second here, look at the dates. This was ten years ago! It's an old story about an old case."

I knew that. "Maybe new guys are on it."

"You don't want us to go," he said. "Okay, say so, but don't be sneaky."

I hadn't even known how much I didn't want them to do it. "Just watching out for you," I said.

How giddy they were about the first trip. Wiley and Maxwell and Claude loaded the car with Cheetos and Fritos and Pepsi and beer, with JAY-Z blasting from the dashboard, and they were ready for six hours of male partying on the road. And when they came home three days later, they had goofy stories about the supplier's quirks; a trunk packed with Winstons, Camels, Marlboros, and Parliaments; and they were full of themselves.

Boyd was the one who did the selling in New York, who got the stuff into bodegas and newsstands. He had his own way of chatting with some manager about how people kept smoking, health or no health, working his way into the offer: let me know what you need. Just for favorite customers. And he supplied some of the guys who sold packs out of big black garbage bags on 125th Street. Until he moved them on out, those long boxes of cigarettes were stacked in my closets and filed under my bed. "Not against the law to possess tobacco," he said.

•

Wiley was the one who worried about the car. "It's a workhorse, but you got to baby it," he said. He took it to be washed, he checked its oil, he inspected its insides like a doctor. His private goal in life was to one day own a Mercedes. He said the Germans made the best cars; everyone knew that. "Don't laugh," he said. "It could happen."

The profits were rolling in much faster than I expected. Boyd bought us a really gigantic TV with the proceeds. Oliver was thrilled to pieces, and I didn't mind either. Oliver had sneakers that lit up and a kiddie electric guitar, I had a new leather jacket for spring, and the refrigerator was full of leftovers in cartons from whatever food place we liked that week. I now lived in a household where stress about money was a thing of the past. A lighthearted zone.

The boys, of course, had to keep going back to Virginia. They seemed to like it, week by week. Boyd envied them. "It'll get old," I said. "All the time in the car. Like a family vacation that keeps starting over." Wiley liked to brag about those Virginia girls, hotter than you'd think, and Claude had actually met someone named Darisse that he spoke about more and more.

"She's not like girls here, they always complain, whatever you do," he said. "Once she decides she likes you, she's on your side all the way. That's her, that's the way she is."

The others teased him about how he eager he always was to get to Virginia. Wiley said, "You do not want to get in the way of a man and where his dick is leading. Almost knocked me over once just getting out of the car when we finally got to Richmond."

They liked Richmond. From repeated success, from tests passed and suspense endured, their personalities were all showing signs of change. Claude had stopped looking hangdog and was now a seemlier specimen, Maxwell took on the dignity of a general, and Wiley was getting closer to unbearable. Boyd simply had more hope in him.

They all had their agendas. Their projects. Claude gave Lynnette a chunk of money to visit their ex-junkie mother in Philadelphia and take her out, show her a good time. Wiley was always buying spectacular clothes for his several girlfriends. Boyd was saving up, sort of, to get a better apartment for us, one his probation board would approve.

Boyd was still at the diner, for his probation officer's sake. He said when people gave him tips now, he thought, *You think I want this chump change?* But he was professional, slipping the pittance into his pocket. What a charade. For the trips to Virginia, Maxwell carried a briefcase filled with cash, and I helped Boyd count and pack the layers of different denominations.

And I was in my own disguise at the vet's office, a princess performing humble tasks without complaint. Dogs and cats gave me their panicked gazes or looked away, and I thought, *Be brave, sometimes things turn out much better than you can tell.* All the technicians said I was very bubbly these days and liked to ask if I'd gotten into the acepromazine, used for anxious dogs.

They thought my mood was about a man, not about money. One of the receptionists told the other I was an "expert" in men. Obviously, I had talked too much, recounted too long a list. By that gauge, the years since puberty were peaks and valleys and stretches of incoherent landscape. There was Oliver's father, Kelvin, who turned out to be much worse than I thought and whom I left when I was pregnant, and Tony, the one I'd first run off with, whom my father hated because he was a teenage drunk but whom I loved for a long time. And there was a bunch of perfectly nice hookups I couldn't be expected to remember very well. Boyd was the best, even if I hadn't always known it.

The runs to Virginia had developed a kind of order, through the professional intensities of Maxwell and Boyd. I was as thrilled as anyone by the sight of all that money, bills and bills, when I helped Boyd pack the briefcase. "Gorgeous, isn't?" Boyd said. "Don't get distracted."

Claude was the one appointed to pick up the cash, and he was the world's gladdest errand boy. He'd walk in the door saying, "Here to get my greens," or "You got that nice black leather satchel for me?" One nice day in late June he came in so cheerful his face was like a kid's, all shifting smirks and laughing eyes.

"Guess what?" he said. "I get to drive. Wiley the man is nowhere to be found, so I am the one."

"What do you mean, nowhere?" Boyd said.

"Called his phone, buzzed his doorbell. Gone goodbye. In bed with some bitch is everybody's guess."

"You can't drive."

"I *am* driving. That's how it is."

"You never even been on a highway," Boyd said. "I'll do it. If I have to, I have to. Don't move, okay? I'm phoning Maxwell."

"Fuck this shit," Claude said.

Boyd went into the bedroom so we couldn't hear. Claude and I stood around like two lumps of different fear.

"Okay, listen," Boyd came back to tell us. "The operation is suspended for another two hours. Either Wiley turns up, or I step in. You want to talk to Maxwell?"

Whatever Maxwell said depressed Claude and made him agree.

I didn't say it till Claude was gone. "This is a total fucking mistake. You get stopped on the highway for anything at all, you're violating probation. They can send you right back in."

"They hardly ever do that."

"You're such an expert. Wait a few days, for Christ's sake," I said. "They can get a different driver."

"You have no idea whatsoever how business works. You don't show up with the supply, people find someone else."

I saw then that I was going to spend the best years of my life visiting Boyd at Rikers. Or much worse places. Oliver would grow older, and we'd be there in those rooms.

"I'm begging you," I said. "You want me on my knees? Is that what you want?"

"Oh, Reyna," he said. "Don't do that."

I did almost get down and do it. I'd been on my knees in lust, but to kneel to plead with him, what would that mean?

"You know I'm right," I said.

"Can't be just anyone who drives, has to be someone we trust."

"Like Wiley was so fine."

"Till now he was."

"Get someone better."

"Yeah, yeah. You could, you know."

"What?"

A great sorrow had crossed his face. "Can you do it, baby?"

Boyd was the one pleading. My own skin flushed from the shock of it, and then I was flattered. He thought I could do it. Which I could. Drive six hours to Virginia—who cared? Me to the rescue. For Boyd I could do it. I could use my own body to block him from idiocy.

Except that I was a mother. Boyd was already thinking through that part of it. He'd go pick up Oliver later—Oliver would be thrilled to share a pizza and watch movies tonight, guys together, and Boyd could get someone to cover the breakfast shift at the diner tomorrow. Daycare already had Boyd on the list, authorized adult. No problem. By late tomorrow night I'd be home. Oliver would hardly notice.

What was I thinking? I was packing. Toothbrush, T-shirt, was it sweltering hot in Virginia now? I could hang out at the motel pool (I hoped it had a pool) while the boys did the buying. What I wanted was Boyd falling all over himself in gratitude, which he wasn't doing. He was all business, calling Maxwell to explain, changing the motel rooms. "Hey," he said from the phone, "they're stocking up for the ride, you want your Diet Sprite?" But when I stood at the door with my red suitcase and my big floppy hat for the sun, Boyd said, "I wish you didn't have to do this." We had a long, desperate hug—I liked how noble and useful I was about to be, and he did too, I knew.

They weren't ready for me when I got to Maxwell's. What a mess that apartment was. Pizza cartons in the living room, used towels across the couch, TV on full blast. Technically Boyd still lived here but hardly.

"We got the expert here," Claude said, flicking his head in my direction. "You're not with the dogs?"

"I only work some days," I said.

"She can drive fast," Maxwell said. "Reyna the Rapid. That's what Boyd said. We're late already."

Speeding White Woman Stopped on Highway with Two Colored Fellows. Or was that just the old South? Richmond was a black-majority town, and the boys were always talking about how great the bars were. The trip back was the one to worry about, with the car loaded.

"You got the first aid kit?" Maxwell said.

Claude was full of high amusement about this. He flipped open the top of a white plastic box to show me the contents—wrapped in a green jeweler's cloth was something metal. A gun. A pistol, with a blunt nose and curved grip, in two tones of steel, dark and light. It took the breath out of me, as if they'd shown me a pet snake. Why was I so fucking surprised?

"Goes in the glove compartment," Maxwell said. "You're okay with us, you know? Protected."

I was out of my depth. I was a dopey girl with a sun hat.

"Everybody ready?" Maxwell said. "We're late."

And then we were walking down the block to where the car was parked. Claude had the bag of snacks and we all dragged our wheelies, tourists on parade.

"Next time, *I* drive," Claude said.

"Ignore him," Maxwell said.

"Hurry up, my girl is waiting," Claude said.

We were standing in front of the car, which needed a wash and who knew what else. Maxwell was fishing in his pockets for his copy of the key.

I might've just gotten in, when he opened the door—it wasn't beyond me—but why was I going on this armed and half-assed felony of an errand? Why would someone like me want to do this? I'd made a fake decision, I'd lied to myself.

"You know," I said, "I think I've had a change of mind about this."

"Little late for that," Maxwell said. "You want to say what's wrong?"

Claude, of course, was cursing all my female body parts in a hiss of boiling outrage. Fucking cunt, all bullshit all the time, ugly sneaky twat, he told Boyd a long time ago.

"Listen, Reyna," Maxwell said. "So you're nervous, okay, first time, but you'll see, always happens we have fun on these trips." He kept at it for a while, the delights of Virginia, and I might've done it, after all, if Claude had shut up. I froze, I didn't move, I just shook my head.

In the end, Maxwell said, "I hate this crap," which meant he'd given up. Claude got into the driver's seat and said, "We're out of here, fuck you, we're flying, heading into the sunset, you know?" The car made a coughing noise, and then he got it going. And there I was, on Lenox Avenue, with my perky red suitcase. I walked the fifteen blocks back to my apartment. Boyd was gone, picking up Oliver, as I'd hoped. By the time he got back, my guess was they'd have phoned him from the car, he'd know.

I lay on the sofa, gutted and wasted by what I'd done, and I couldn't even move when Oliver dashed in—"Hey, Mommy, hey!"—followed by Boyd, whose face was a death mask and who didn't say a word.

Oliver was jumping on my stomach. Boyd leaned forward to murmur in my ear, "What the fuck did you ever care about?" and he was out the door before I even knew.

The hot feel of his breath was still in my ear. What good did my loving Boyd do either of us? He was never coming back. Love was nothing, love was a vapor.

I had to feed Oliver his supper, and he was upset because I'd almost left him and then I hadn't. Oh, he didn't want anything I offered; he screeched against all of it. "Forget it," I said. "Suit yourself." I was seeing all too clearly what I'd done. I'd humiliated Boyd in front of his friends. I'd tricked him and disgraced him. Only Claude was happy now, behind the wheel. Maybe he'd take my side.

I didn't hear a word from Boyd or any of them for five days. I could phone all I wanted, no answer. On the sixth day I came home from work and I heard a rustle in the bedroom, and there was Boyd packing his clothes into a big piece of luggage. He didn't even look up. "It's worse than you think," he said. "You don't know what's gone down."

I didn't know that outside Baltimore Claude had tried to turn onto I-95 from a rest stop and he'd collided with a truck, smashed into it so hard that he died with his seat belt on before an ambulance even got there. Maxwell was a mess, he was still in the hospital, but he was okay.

I followed Boyd's voice, dry as sand, and I sobbed as loud as an adult ever sobs. Boyd put his arm around me stiffly, he did his best, as if I were a relative he wasn't crazy for. "You got to watch out for Lynnette," he said. "She's all broken up and she doesn't like you."

They'd had the funeral already. The mother from Philadelphia had made an unholy racket and Lynnette had been like a ghost, all sedated. In the days since then she seemed to have to talk to everyone nonstop, phoning at all hours, showing up whenever. "Shouldn't have taken her off those drugs so soon."

The stiff hug was over. I was a wreck of smeared tears. We looked at each other, bowed down with horror at all of it. I wanted to think he was sorry to lose me. I was in the grip of a longing to go back in time, to undo what I'd done, and this wish was slashing my innards.

After Boyd left, I wanted to ask about the funeral—which church? What could any minister have said over Claude? A boy so unformed and goofy and shallow that dying seemed deeper than anything he'd know how to do. Who had told the girl in Richmond, or was she still waiting?

And the money was probably still in the car. In whatever junkyard the car had been hauled to. All their cleverness had come to nothing—Claude, of course, had never been the clever part. But he might've smartened up, in time. If this accident hadn't killed him, it might have taught him.

They had kept me from even a back seat in the church. Boyd could have argued for me, if he'd wanted, except that I'd put him in a bad spot too. I was like someone who sets a fire by mistake: not her fault but it is her fault.

Oliver kept asking where Boyd was. "Away for a while," I said. I didn't believe in lying to children but it was too hard to explain, your mother didn't know herself as well as she thought she did, so someone died, and Boyd doesn't like it.

On the street a few nights later I saw Lynnette at the crosswalk, stepping out ahead of me. She was looking very skinny in purple leggings and she was talking nonstop, as Boyd had described, holding forth to some guy walking with her. She was so intent she didn't see me, and I could hear her rasping, "Not gonna take that shit," over and over. Her voice was hoarse and crazy-sounding (the woman was in mourning, she was entitled), and I was afraid of her.

One afternoon when I came into work at the vet's, the girl who was on the front desk told me a man had come in asking for me and hadn't left his name. What did he look like? "African American," she said, "in a T-shirt." Not much of a description. It might be Maxwell, but he'd be bruised or bandaged if he was out by now. It wasn't Boyd, who had my phone number and could just call. One of Claude's friends? I didn't like it.

It might be nothing. It might be a happy pet owner wanting to thank me for past niceness. I was edgy all day, on guard every time I had to buzz someone in. I lived in a mist of dread, didn't I, and I didn't know how to guess about things. Nothing happened that day but when I went home I told Oliver I had a summer plan for us.

My aunt had gone off to Cape Cod with her friend, Pat, and how long was she going to be gone? I was wondering if it might not be a good idea to apartment-sit for Kiki, get out of my neighborhood. I told my father I wanted

Oliver nearer the playgrounds downtown, which were safer. (This was a racist fib—the playgrounds near us were fine.)

Kiki sounded cheerful when I called her. She was having great walks on the beach, eating fried clams and that great Portuguese soup—did I still have a key? I did. "Well, just go right over," she said. "Of course." I promised not to let Oliver trash the place.

"You always think I trash things," Oliver said, while I was talking. "It's not me."

I thought of Claude every day. His shambling self had been released into the world, to wait outside every bodega, lope around every corner. If anyone had unfinished business, he did. If anyone needed more time, he did. He was going to wander for years at the edge of my line of sight.

When I moved into Kiki's apartment with Oliver, the hardest part was trying to carry enough of his toys. Her place was much less modern than where we lived, homier, more lopsided. I was comforted by the cluttered kitchen with its hanging pots, by the Turkish carpet with its Kiki-history. I made a big game out of bedding Oliver down on the living room futon, and he was sort of okay. At night, under Kiki's sheets, I missed Boyd in secret desperation, Boyd who was never coming back and who was farther away than ever. I didn't think this was the worst of it—that I'd lost Boyd—but knowing that didn't make it any less bitter.

•

The day I took the long subway ride back up to my apartment in Harlem to get more clothes, I walked in and wondered all over again if any cash had been left behind. I looked in the freezer; I looked in all the drawers; I looked in the top of the toilet tank. But Boyd had taken it, if there'd been any left.

How pleased both of us had been, in our glory days. I was innocent then of what I knew about myself, where showing off could go. That was over, that innocence. If I ever found any money in the house, I'd send it straight to Lynnette.

I would, too. Claude would want every bit of it sent to his sister—Lynnette was always broke. She had a job, but it barely kept her above water. She was a "beauty technician," which meant she plucked people's eyebrows and extended their lashes.

I wouldn't let Lynnette near *my* eyes, but customers probably wanted her; she could be flashy in a fabulous way. Once, for Claude's birthday, she wore rhinestone earrings long as bananas and a polo shirt with lights on it that spelled out *CLAUDE*. Claude said her outfit made her look like Times Square. It was his twenty-fourth birthday.

Boyd had toasted him with some ridiculous birthday rap. *Got to say it loud, power to the Claude.* And would Boyd and I get to meet again in this life? Maybe sixty years from now. It was hard to think of Boyd old, but I could do it, I could picture him gray and gaunt, looking out from an armchair, braving the worst. I knew how he'd be; I knew him. He'd be glad to see me by then, more than glad. I could feel myself wishing it were that time now.

Part II

3

When Claude didn't show up at the bar, Darisse was plenty upset. She was all dolled up, as her grandmother would say, in a little itty-bitty skirt and a halter top and her hair gelled into a loop. Where was Claude? She walked up and down; she peered around the tables in the back. He never came late, however long it took to drive from New York to Richmond. No sign of his friends anywhere in the bar either. The place was packed, but she looked hard. No answer to her texts. She rang and she just got his message, over and over.

People were known to change their minds. Say one thing, do another. Could happen. The guy who smiled all over himself when he saw her? The guy who sent her hot love texts every single day? Maybe he panicked because he'd fallen for her so hard. Maybe being too crazy about her scared the shit out of him. None of her girlfriends were buying that explanation. Darisse didn't either, by the end of the night. She tried not to drink too much but she was tearful by the last message she left him. *Wr r u at?*

Darisse knew that things fell apart, nothing lasted forever; she knew this better than most people bothered to. Her working life was all about natural decay—she worked for a hospice service as a home health aide, washing, watching, spooning, combing, cleaning as people got worse. Everyone always wanted to know how she could stand to do it. But it was much better than a lot of other crap people did. She did it with respect; she got respect. A lot of jobs nobody really needed you to do.

Claude said, "All the old men, don't they try to grope you? I would. You bet." Darisse said they only sent her out to ladies and they weren't all old either. She gave them sponge baths in bed; she knew all their crevices and sores and sadness of flesh. Everybody had bodies; she wasn't afraid of bodies. Not with Claude either. His sleek sweet shape, his speedy impulses and wild susceptibility. But now he'd met someone else he liked better. That was what her friends said.

Darisse's grandmother was not happy when she got home so late that night. She woke up when Darisse came in and stood in the hallway of the apartment, with her hair all crazy and her eyes puffed into squints. "You could get yourself killed," she said, "wandering around at this hour. Get murdered by me for waking me up." She turned and went back to her room.

Darisse had a number of reasons for not wanting to get on her bad side. Even on good days, her grandmother was grouchy and hard to deal with, but she loved Darisse and hadn't hesitated all that long when Darisse turned up out of the blue asking for a place to stay. But she'd put her foot down about taking in any kids as well. Anybody know how many babies she'd raised? No more babies in the house. New rule, spread the word. So most of the time Darisse's two-year-old, Jeshauna, was with Lionel's mother. She got decent care, but Lionel, Darisse's ex, was the gatekeeper. He got to decide when Darisse saw her and when she didn't, and he had his ways of deciding.

When Darisse woke up the next day, her grandmother was already in church. Darisse didn't do church (that was her right), but when she checked her phone and there was nothing on it, she wanted to pray: *Send me Claude.* You could wish; it wasn't hypocrisy to wish.

In her miserable, no-good jalopy that ate up too much gas, she drove to the motel where Claude and his boys always stayed. The car they liked so much, the silver Taurus, wasn't there. She went to the desk and said, "I'd just like to leave a message," and she gave them Wiley's name. They used his name for bookings because he had the driver's license. No such gentleman was registered.

•

"What, are you stalking them now?" her friend Frances said. "Let it go. He turns up, let him talk. But forget it for now."

Darisse saw the practicality in this but she knew what she knew about Claude. He didn't have real secrets but he had a different nature than people thought. He was saving up to rent his sister a whole salon for her business. He was going to buy her—Darisse—a set of gold earrings as big as Hula-Hoops. He'd never met Jeshauna but when he came to Richmond the time before last he brought a tiny electric piano for her. She liked it too; she banged on it like a little lunatic.

Amanda, who was Darisse's current hospice patient, said a two-year-old was too young for electric toys, but Darisse said, "I watch her. Most people don't trouble themselves to watch their kids."

"You're a good mother," Amanda said, in her whooshy voice. She thought Jeshauna lived with her, and Darisse didn't say otherwise.

Amanda was forty-seven, with advanced lung cancer and no children (hence the need for Darisse). There was a husband who came in at night, a paunchy guy with a blond goatee, very nice. He was a maintenance supervisor at the university, where Amanda had been a secretary. They lived in tract housing, on a lane of ranch-style homes that looked like motel units, beyond the outskirts of the city. Amanda was local; her father had once worked in a Philip Morris factory.

Claude, carrier of trunkfuls of Marlboros, Newports, Parliaments, and even Basics, didn't smoke himself, never had. Amanda, who breathed with the help of a machine more and more of the time, said she still had dreams of lighting up a cigarette and was very disappointed to wake up without one. She hated the tobacco companies, who were glad to kill her for a profit—hate was not even the word. But most people were no better than that if you wagged a dollar at them. "Not you," she said. "You don't make money."

This was true. Darisse got only a fraction of what the agency charged for her. But she got as much work as she wanted; people asked for Darisse, they wrote letters saying she was an angel on earth, they told friends to make sure they got her and no one else. For what she did, she was doing okay. When someone like Claude came along (actually no one like him had come before), she was thrilled by the gifts and the promises—who wouldn't be?—and she naturally started thinking about what being with him more might mean. If she had a chunk of money in her hand, she could get Lionel to give her Jeshauna back. Might not take that much. And Claude always said, "No nickel-and-diming when you with me." *Had* said. She'd heard him say it but it was becoming very much like something she'd made up.

She checked Claude's Facebook page, which he hadn't done anything to for a year. There was an old photo of a birthday party, a slinky woman in a T-shirt with *CLAUDE* spelled out in lights (didn't the shirt get hot?). He'd shown her those photos. If Darisse could remember the sister's name, maybe she could find her.

All people had names, but theirs was Johnson. No good searching for that one. And how could the Internet bring him to her, if he wasn't showing up on his own two feet? She had no luck remembering Maxwell's full name, but Wiley had the world's most asinine picture on Facebook, his face twisted up like a drunk monster. Darisse asked to friend him.

If Claude was in police custody, if he was in the hospital, wouldn't his name show up in a newspaper? Not in the Richmond *Times-Dispatch*, not in the Richmond *Free Press* either. Not on Google. She was doing what she could, not just waiting, working her smartphone harder than it wanted to work. Who did he think he was? She talked to him in her mind. *You can stop messing with me. You can tell me. Whatever it is. Hurry up.*

A person can check her phone only so many times. Day after day. The worst part was at the end of the week when she called and the mechanical voice answered at once, without ringing first. Sign of a used-up battery. Maybe he had a new phone now. Maybe he was in another city. She was still here and he knew goddamn well where she was.

At the end of the second week something changed in her. She understood very well that when you took a good look under a clear, hard light, the world was a fucked-up hellhole. Most people knew this, she'd known this, but nobody wanted to think about it all the time. It didn't pay to forget for too long.

At work she wasn't any different. She laughed when Amanda made her usual crack, "The way my health is, don't go buying me any unripe bananas." Amanda was repeating it for the benefit of a new nurse, who'd come to check the equipment. The nurse said, "Oh, you can buy a few pounds. You've got more time." The nurse was a guy in his thirties, short and sober-faced, with a shaved head (how many black men still thought that was sexy?). There were more male nurses now, and they weren't all gay either.

Darisse thought Amanda had a few months more, and she was often (but not always) right. So far Amanda only needed morphine at night, when her husband could shoot one of those teeny syringes in her mouth. Darisse wasn't allowed. "He was scared the first time," Amanda said, "but then he got the hang of it." People had to get used to things or else. Darisse had seen *else* and did not think well of it.

The male nurse was named Silas and he knew what he was doing. You could tell in about a second. He got the oxygen machine set up closer to where Amanda liked to sit, he talked to her and not just to her husband, who'd come home early for this. He said, "You people are doing well. I see that. In the situation."

Darisse had heard them squabble but Fred the husband was good most of the time. He held Amanda's arm when she took steps; he called her Honey. Would Claude ever do as well for her if she was sick? She could imagine it, but a person could imagine anything.

Darisse walked the nurse to the door. "Very nice to meet you," he said, more warmly than he had to. He probably looked better out of the white smock. She herself was in green, with those ugly matching pants. Never mind.

On Friday she got to Lionel's mother's house exactly at five, because he could be a real prick if she was late. Lionel opened the door and said, "You come here dressed like a janitor, in those green things. What's that going to mean to Jeshauna?"

"What's she know about janitors?"

Jeshauna, who heard her voice, began screeching in excitement from inside the house. Lionel's mother was saying, "It's okay, baby. Don't have to scream."

Lionel just stared. "I should make you go home and change into something decent."

Darisse didn't talk about it. She just stood there.

"Next time you look better, okay?"

Once Darisse got past the hallway she was stormed by Jeshauna, the world's fastest toddler. Darisse scooped her up and said, "Princess girl." There she was, chunky body, pointed chin, round soulful eyes, at last. Lionel's mother had put her hair in cornrows with tiny pink barrettes.

Darisse always thought that she braided it too tight for such a little kid but Jeshauna never complained.

Lionel's mother had packed a backpack large enough for a whole kindergarten, and Darisse had to put it on and carry it to the car while she pushed Jeshauna in her stroller. The weight of no-Claude was still on her, but she could get lively for Jeshauna. She had to do some degree of acting at her job, keeping the more useless forms of despair under the rug, and she could certainly do as much for her own girl.

And the weekend went very well. Jeshauna, who was almost three now, picked over her French fries at McDonald's with her usual obsessive rapture, and later she was content watching cartoons on a tablet in the small, dark bedroom that was Darisse's. She did fine with Darisse's grandmother when they were all in the kitchen at breakfast—she sang a tuneless nonsense song for her, and Darisse's grandmother laughed in appreciation, which she didn't always do. The weather was sunny and not too hot all weekend. Frances brought sandwiches on Sunday and they had a picnic by the river, with Jeshauna running around the playground so much that she actually tired herself out. They napped together, back in Darisse's room, and Darisse dreamed something about Claude that wasn't good. And it was late when she woke up—she had to hustle them both to get back to Lionel fast. "Why're you always so slow? You do it on purpose," she yelled at Jeshauna. And they didn't get to his house till eight fifteen instead of seven.

•

Lionel's mother had a house that had been her father's, a narrow two-story wood-frame on the edge of Jackson Ward. Lionel had set up his own apartment in the basement, but he was out on the porch when Darisse pulled up. The last time she was late he'd cut her back to three weekends a month. "Waiting waiting waiting," he said, though she'd phoned from the car. His mother, who didn't hate Darisse, beckoned her in and took the sleeping Jeshauna from her arms. Kids slept through any number of things.

Lionel said, "You never change."

"We fell asleep, wasn't on purpose. You know that. Listen, I'm sincerely sorry," she said. This was a code between them.

Sincerity meant a favor. After he took the backpack into the house and came out again, she followed him around to the back entrance to his apartment. When he flicked on the light they were in his living room, which had an old red sofa and a straw rug from somewhere; he'd made an effort. They sat on the couch together and she put her hand on his knee.

He took her hand and put it on his crotch, with a faint smile on his face, a teasing look, and she rubbed him with the flat of her palm. This had been her idea, this strategy, when he first decided to start making rules about when she could and couldn't see Jeshauna. Darisse had very little to bargain with and had in fact been relieved to come up with this. Now she waited while he unzipped his pants, and she leaned toward him and went down on her knees. He liked seeing her kneel, she could

tell. Once she had loved sex any way they did it, once she
had loved him. Now his body had a different meaning;
the hardness and the taste of him were not stairways to
heaven but a kind of work. But it was nothing, to do for
her kid. People did much more than this. She felt him
growing and moving under her tongue and there was
some triumph for her in that. It kept him from having
all the cards, if you wanted to look at it that way, though
most people wouldn't.

She'd done this just once after meeting Claude, and that
had been in the very early days, when Claude was just a
new rush of excitement. And it wasn't entirely bad then to
have Claude to think of, no matter what Lionel was doing.
She liked having her own precious secret. Now, as Lionel
began to thrust inside her mouth, she did feel like weeping.
A person as sad as she was shouldn't have to do this. And
there was more work in this part of it, so she began to feel
that she was after all betraying Claude. Doing too much.
She went on with it, what was the point in stopping?

When she drove home that night, she was thinking too
much about what Claude would've thought if he'd known.
Maybe he did know, maybe he'd been told by Lionel,
maybe that was why he was gone. Not that she ever said a
word about her private life to Lionel, but Richmond wasn't
that big a place—someone could've mentioned seeing her,
saying she had this New York guy now. But it wasn't like
Lionel to take that much trouble to spite her. He wasn't

Joan Silber

given to big evil gestures or tricky plots, he was lazy. She was just making up a story now, getting stuck in her own mind.

It was only a short drive back to her grandmother's, over the other side of the highway to Gilpin Court, a neighborhood nobody was rushing to gentrify. Darisse had spent half of her childhood in this same apartment, in a low-rise housing project on one of the bare and treeless blocks. She was safe here, she often said, because people knew her, but her grandmother always snorted, "Yeah, safe, right."

Maybe Claude had been shot. No one had suggested it, but he could've been on the wrong corner at the wrong time; he didn't know Richmond and his friends didn't either. And maybe it was true that gangs were moving in to control the cigarette routes. Maybe Claude and the others hadn't known what they were getting into. Even she could tell they were bullshitting half the time.

Silas the nurse came back that week to check on how the plan of care was being implemented and see how the supplies were holding out. "What kind of name," Amanda said, "is Silas?" She was pausing longer for breath these days.

"In the Bible," he said, "he goes traveling around preaching with Paul. They get locked in prison but an earthquake breaks their chains and opens the door."

"Are you religious?" Darisse asked.

"Not me," he said, "but my parents, oh, yes."

Darisse was secretly becoming more religious, but in private; she had her own rituals. She sat on her bed with her eyes closed; she thought of the walls of the room turning into air. Air from a larger space. The point was to ask for strength. Improvement wasn't coming any other way. She was doing this almost every night and there was an aftereffect that pleased her.

"I had to go to Sunday school," Amanda wheezed, "when I was little. And Bible camp too. You wouldn't believe. What we got up to. At Bible camp."

Silas said, "Nothing more exciting than what you're not supposed to do."

"I see that all the time with my daughter," Darisse said. "Just say no and she wants it big-time."

Shit. She didn't make a habit of telling men right away that she had a kid.

Silas (why would he care anyway?) was writing out his report. Amanda said, "Were your parents upset when you left the church?"

"I still play keyboard in church on Sundays," he said. "Keeps everybody happy. We don't talk about how I play in bars too."

"What bars?" Darisse said.

"Just every now and then. Not so often."

"I think that's wonderful," Amanda said.

"What bars?" Darisse said.

•

It wasn't even a bar she had ever heard of, but that was the beginning. Some friends of his who weren't bad at all were playing next week, in case she ever wanted to go hear music. She might just. They said this at the door and he took her number into his phone. "Well," he said, "we will talk."

It turned out to be jazz, which she wasn't crazy for, but so what? When he picked her up at the apartment, he was wearing a pressed shirt in a silvery gray color, a big upgrade from his scrubs. He shook her grandmother's hand—how old was he? That was the first thing she asked him in the car. "Guess," he said.

Thirty-two, ten years older than she was. Probably an ex-wife somewhere, maybe getting alimony from him. When they walked into the club, they had to shut up while the music played, strangers though they still were. The music sounded too thick, too much going on at once, until all the playing cleared for the piano and she could follow a tune as it twisted around beautifully. But she didn't know why people applauded after—what had just happened? She told him she liked it.

By the time the music was over she'd had too many drinks but she could keep it together. (She never had to keep anything together for Claude.) Was Silas from Richmond? Yes, but he'd lived in Charlotte; his kids (uh-huh) were still in Charlotte with their mom. "Amanda thinks you're smarter than the doctor," Darisse said. They weren't actually supposed to talk about patients outside the job.

"Nice lady," he said.

Darisse was thinking, *Hope she stays nice.* You couldn't ever tell how people were going to get. She'd had one man, ninety years old and pale as a fish (she'd lied to Claude about not being sent to men), who was prone to what the agency called racial epithets. And there was a darling African American granny who accused her of stealing.

Silas wanted to know how long she'd been a home health aide, did she like it? And did she plan to work for herself someday instead of the agency? She hated this part, the conversation that was like an interview. She missed Claude very much in the midst of this.

"I might move to New York," she said.

"You want some place bigger?" he said. "I can understand that."

"Maybe I just have to make my own head bigger," she said.

She didn't mean that either, but they got to talking about hat sizes—he wore a 7-3/8? really? his head didn't look that large—and hats they had loved. Baltimore Orioles for him, for her a white flowered concoction she'd worn for church as a child.

Then they had to go meet his friends, who were standing at the bar by now, had to tell them how great they'd been. The drummer looked old enough to be everybody's father; the others were Silas's age. They shook her hand. Silas wanted to know why they changed the bass solo on "Willow Weep" and what fool did the sound check. And that was the rest of the night.

But at the very end, when he walked to her door, there

was a real kiss—a sudden revelation of him in tongue and lip. She hadn't even expected it, and she was glad for herself then, proud. Not such a bad evening after all. Okay, okay, something was going to happen. Another date—that was how he did things. One step at a time.

The next week unfolded, day after day, and where were his phone calls? Nothing nothing. She was sick of making guesses about the motives of men. She hadn't been totally sure she liked him anyway.

In her phone were still the texts Claude had sent her. Some of the old ones had slipped out of sight, but *Cant cant wait 2 c u* was there if she wanted to look at it, which she did. And several *MUSL*'s, missing you shitloads. The texts were from weeks and weeks ago, an era now very distant, buried in the past, over long since. But reading them was irresistible because joy still lurked in the compressed words, and it wasn't fake joy.

She took Jeshauna to church with her on their next weekend. Her grandmother was delighted (not something Darisse saw often) and ironed Jeshauna's dress before they went. Jeshauna was pretty good in church—she liked the singing, everyone liked the singing. All the swaying, all the surging choruses. Darisse only hoped she didn't catch the words to "Were You There When They Crucified My Lord?" which had too much violence for a little kid.

Jeshauna's good behavior didn't last all the way to the sermon, and Darisse walked her out to the hallway and whispered her down from too much loudness. She put a game on the tablet for her.

The minister's voice, gravelly and full, came through to Darisse over Jeshauna's babbling. He was talking about how Bathsheba was married to Uriah the Hittite (the what?) but King David saw her in the bath and lusted for her and when she got pregnant afterward he sent her husband into the frontlines to get killed. And was David punished for this? He was. The infant died soon after birth. And years later his beloved son Absalom led a civil war against him, and to show his right to the throne he had sexual intercourse in public with ten of his father's concubines.

It said that in the Bible? What an ugly story. "What do we take from this?" the minister said. "One, nobody gets away with anything. Not kings. Two, Jesus Christ is from the House of David. He came out of *that*."

Darisse had gone expecting something a lot sweeter and wasn't sure church had been such a great idea. Afterward her grandmother stood around in the foyer where the cake was set out, gabbing (probably about her) with the other hat-ladies, and Jeshauna was picking the icing off her piece.

Darisse already knew the part about nobody getting away with anything. Every mistake of hers had come back to bite her. In her teenage days she'd stolen Lionel from her friend Vanessa, and it hadn't been easy either. And look how that worked out. In the first months after her daughter was born, she wasn't the best mother; she turned away too often, she minded too much the way a baby had to be, reaching and needing. Now she'd give everything she had to be with Jeshauna more.

On the way home from church Jeshauna was allowed to eat a whole packet of cookies while she sat in her stroller, because she'd just been so good. Even Darisse's grandmother said so.

Maybe church helped (oh, she didn't believe that), because that very Sunday night she got a phone call from what's-his-name Silas. They were short in the hospice service unit and he'd been working extra shifts and the time just got away from him, he meant to call sooner. Whatever.

But the next date with him was better. They went to a movie they both thought was funny; they drank beer and ate chicken wings and looked each other over. "I like these movies where people do stupid things," she said (the leading man had thrown a briefcase full of cash into the wrong car), "and you get to laugh instead of just wanting to yell at them."

"Sometimes the audience yells," he said. "That's a good audience."

"That guy was so stupid!"

"People think they're so smart and then they're not," he said. "That's the plot of all funny movies, right there. Don't you think?"

Darisse thought her own life fit this story line but she

kept this notion to herself. Tonight he was wearing a navy blue shirt with a texture of stripes in the fabric. She never would've guessed he was any kind of dresser, and he'd picked this out from his closet for the date with her.

What kind of money did nurses make? Decent but medium, right? You'd think Silas had more, from the way his apartment was. When he turned on the light she saw a big shining dining room table and a whole field of orchids along a window. He liked orchids. But she wasn't there to admire the furnishings. He brought her a glass of water from the kitchen and she drank it while she was still standing up. "Delicious water," she said, and then he moved toward her.

What surprised her was the way they just fell into it. She would've said (had said to Frances) that they were both hesitant, still making up their minds, so now she was startled by the lush fever of it. Unexpected too were the signs he gave of being tickled to death about what was happening, about the good news of her; he sighed and kept lapsing into sexy chuckles. Well, that was nice.

By the time they got to the bedroom, there was a surge of happiness in her to be doing all this again. This was the next phase of her life; here it was already. *I'm landing on my feet*, she thought, all the while they were actually having sex, this was sex. He showed off a little and then he paid attention; she could feel him guessing about her. They did very well together, through most of it.

•

In the morning when the alarm rang she thought she was
in jail—she'd never been in jail, but the sound was so jar-
ring she dreamed herself there. When she woke again,
Silas was in his scrubs and had brought her a toaster waf-
fle on a plate with butter and syrup, and a mug of coffee.
"This is the life," she said—she liked waffles—and kissed
his neck, but what she really wanted was to get home fast
and change for work. The bedroom seemed very big and
too full of bright light and too arranged, with its surfaces
of tan and brown and bamboo. On a dresser were the
photos of his kids, a girl and a boy, smiling with their
bicycles.

She might've stolen something, if she were a person
who stole things. Of course, at work she was in houses
stocked with much more expensive things than this one.
But it struck her, as she was getting herself together in
the bathroom, that he trusted her, without that much to
go on.

She got a better look at his street when they went out to
his car. He lived in a big apartment complex, a brick strip
with white columns, a few blocks from the river in what
was still called Tobacco Row, even if tobacco companies
had been out for thirty years. "You think people still get
rich from tobacco?" she said.

"Some do," he said. "They don't feel bad about it
either."

Darisse thought she'd heard of an executive who

repented and crusaded against cigarettes after his wife died of emphysema. But maybe that was just one of those stories.

"Lot of stories in the world," Silas said.

He looked handsome when he said that, one eyebrow raised, and they had a long, solid embrace when they said goodbye in front of her apartment. No, she didn't want him to drive her to work once she got her uniform on— how would she get home without her car? Probably he was in a hurry to get to work too; probably he was just as glad to have the rest of the ride to himself.

Everyone thought she'd fallen into the pie. Frances said, "I'll take him, you don't want him." Her grandmother said, "I like that one; you know I don't say that for nothing." Even Amanda at work (whom she shouldn't have said a thing to) said, "Cute and nice. Big advance over. Your other choices. Just from. What you told me."

Amanda's husband had rigged up a sloping lap desk with a light on it so she could do crossword puzzles while she was lying in bed. The puzzles now just made her sleepy. She wasn't looking at email either, despite the stand her husband had set up with the tablet clamped to it so she couldn't knock it over. The tablet was loaded with a very long playlist of music he was sure she'd like, and sometimes she did like it. He kept wanting to do things.

Everybody thought it was so great that Darisse got phone calls from Silas at least twice a week. Not like

Claude's constant texting (the man had had free time), but Silas was good to talk to; she could go on to him about her grandmother's peculiarities and he would listen.

"Can't expect the same things with each guy," she told Frances. "They all got their own rules."

At her grandmother's house, Darisse hardly went into the kitchen, but Silas liked her to cook with him, with his nice modern appliances. And Jeshauna, although she was cranky and shy at first, took to Silas after he fed her one of those waffles. After that she was hanging on to him whatever he did. "Hey, girl," he would say, "you going to let me move?" She'd have his knee in an arm-lock, but he looked pleased.

His apartment, which wasn't as big as Darisse had thought at first, had that gush of orchids in one window and piles of books about trees (who'd want to read about a tree?), shelves of mystery writers he liked, and a standing keyboard he only played when she wasn't there. He did have music coming at them from speakers a lot of the time, everything from Lil' Kim to Little Richard singing "Hokey Pokey" for Jeshauna. *Put your right foot in.*

Darisse would have gotten word from someone by now if Claude had ever shown himself anywhere in Richmond. There was a chance he and the boys were going to another city (maybe Norfolk?) where somebody was giving them a better deal on cartons of cigarettes; it wouldn't have been Claude who figured that out either. And he hadn't wanted to go to the trouble of telling her, just wanted to leave it the way it was. Just let it go.

She understood she hadn't really known Claude that well. She already knew Silas better. Silas talked more. He made fun of vampire movies, he thought Jesus was some kind of good Communist, he still liked Obama, he rehearsed with his friends every single Thursday night, no exceptions. He didn't mind being an "amateur" musician but his ex-wife had looked down on him for that. Every month he drove four and a half hours to see his kids and sometimes he had them in the summer but not this year. He thought Jeshauna should be in daycare, she needed to be with other kids.

"I could suggest it," Darisse said.

Silas said, "Aren't you the mother?"

Darisse didn't look up from the bowl of cereal she was eating. None of his fucking business. He had no idea.

"I'm just saying," he said.

He had a friend who was a social worker who might be able to make sure she had her rights. Darisse knew plenty of social workers and she wasn't always impressed with them. But maybe.

"When you're ready," he said.

Amanda had long bouts of coughing so heavy it sounded like sobbing. "Fuck this," she'd rasp, when she could speak. She was keeping her personality, at least. She had to be helped onto the commode; she had trouble swallowing. These humiliations caused a look of indignant defeat on her face. "Don't tell Fred. I. Threw up," she'd say.

Fred, the husband, was cutting back on his work hours, coming home earlier. Darisse caught herself starting to wonder how he'd be after Amanda was gone. What would he do with himself, how long would he mourn, would he ever take up with someone else? He would. Men did. Because they could; she didn't blame them.

Amanda got great enjoyment out of teasing Darisse about Silas. Even in her vanishing voice, she liked to kid about how those medical guys knew where all the parts were. Darisse had her act totally ignorant of anything when Silas came for his visit (he always worried about trouble if the agency knew). And after Silas left, they cracked up together, with Amanda choking merrily over every innocent thing Silas said.

But once Darisse and Silas had to work more closely over Amanda, they all stopped pretending anything. They lifted her together to change the bed, they mopped her and let her spit. She looked horrified and embarrassed and said, "Isn't this. Romantic?"

Silas had to keep traveling between patients, which Darisse didn't envy. On the nights when the two of them were really, really tired after work, they got into marathon TV watching. They streamed *Nurse Jackie* and the first season of *Orange Is the New Black* and watched episodes of the old Dave Chappelle show that Silas had on DVD. They

were in a cocoon together, sprawled all over each other on
the couch, eyes reflecting the same images.

Though they'd both grown up mostly in Richmond,
they didn't know any of the same people. Well, Silas was
older. Now he'd met Frances, who came with Darisse the
one time she saw Silas himself play music in a club. They
both thought he was great—he had such a look of concen-
tration, leaning over the keyboard—but he said he was off
and seemed to think poorly of her for not knowing.

Silas's friends—the men he played music with or had
known forever—made sure to talk to her; they asked
what singers she liked and laughed at her stories about
Amanda's unripe bananas. The wives made a show of admiring the way her hair was, how did she do that? She
kept her mouth shut around them, so she didn't sound stupid. Frances talked too much.

Jeshauna was a big fan of Silas. On weekends she slept on
sofa pillows on the floor of his bedroom; she was a good
sleeper. Darisse knew she must be prattling about this to
Lionel's mother and Lionel too, but they hadn't said anything so far. Jeshauna called Silas "Syrah," a name that
might've just gone right by them.

Lionel would just make mean remarks if he knew, but
his mother would want to be nosy about it. And what
would Darisse say? She wouldn't get huffy. Everybody
liked nurses; she only had to say she had a nurse for a
boyfriend. She'd be cool, because being cool was what was

going to get Jeshauna back, once she had enough money for her own place.

She and Silas were getting along well, in bed and out, better than well, but it wasn't going to last forever. This was Darisse's own personal opinion, and not one she'd think of uttering to anyone except maybe Frances. What she said to Frances was, "I don't think we're what you'd call well matched."

"You fighting?" Frances said.

"No, ma'am."

"You're not fighting, you're matched fine."

On Labor Day weekend, Silas drove off to North Carolina to see his kids, but he promised a fun outing the following weekend, all day in the park, their own special holiday. Jeshauna was so excited about this event she insisted on bringing the little toy piano Claude had given her. It wasn't really a whole piano, just a blue plastic keyboard— maybe Silas would hate the clatter of it. But when Darisse set it up on a rock a little ways from the barbecue grounds, he said, "Well, look at this."

It could sound like a drum or a horn and make animal noises too. He had to listen to a barking serenade, Jeshauna's favorite. "Where'd you get this?"

"I found it in the garbage. It's amazing what people throw out." She wasn't going to mention Claude to him.

"Not garbage!" Jeshauna said.

Claude had known the right thing to buy without ever meeting Jeshauna.

Silas got it to play back what Jeshauna banged on it, which Darisse hadn't even known it could do. "These are good," Silas said. "They're cheap as hell but they take a while to break."

Darisse had a terrible urge to pull Jeshauna off the keyboard so she'd never break it.

"Sticking right out of a garbage can," she said.

She could say whatever she wanted; it didn't matter to anyone but her. A person could keep the best of certain private things to herself, so they didn't fade, and she could lie flat-out, when she had to, out of loyalty to what once was. Nothing could get her to take back the lie; she was glad for what she held on to.

"Right in the trash," she said.

4

It wasn't his fault. No one said it was, not even the insurance companies. The Ford Taurus had tear-assed onto the highway and rammed into the side of his tractor-trailer. Teddy remembered the noise of the car's arrival, the unbelievable cosmic smack of it collapsing itself into crumpled metal. The noise fell into an unreal silence in his skull, while he headed his truck to the breakdown lane. After he set out flares, he walked back, with traffic swarming on one side, to peer inside the wreck and see more blood than he knew people had in them, two horror shows of men in mangled poses. He yelled, "Hey! Hello! You okay?" and they didn't answer. Twisted in the seat belts, two young black guys, not moving or making a sound. He stood on the edge of the road, calling 911, trying to sound sane.

He didn't think he smelled gas but maybe he did, and that was when he started shaking. He got one of the car's back doors open and he was trying to drag out the bleeding

passenger—a boy in a Knicks cap, with a bent leg—when
the state cops got there. He'd been afraid the whole time
of fuel leaks catching fire—he would've run and left them
if that had started to happen—and he backed away fast
once he wasn't alone.

Nobody thought it was his fault. The cops made Teddy
fill out diagrams; they checked for skid marks; they wrote
a ticket to the bleeding driver, before the ambulance even
got there. Not his fault, but he knew what he knew. He'd
been thinking of Sally at just that moment, a certain half-
smile she had.

And it turned out nobody was rushing to pay for dam-
ages to the truck, which he actually owned. Word came
soon that the driver of the Taurus who hit him was not
named in the car's insurance policy. This individual—
a kid of twenty-four—couldn't be sued either, since he
never got out of the wrecked car alive. He had gone where
no lawyers could reach him, beyond bills and penalties
and human disputes, beyond all the papers Teddy had
filled out, and he had nothing by way of an estate either.
Teddy's insurance company made a point of checking all
this. And what about the car's owner? Poor as dirt, not
worth suing.

Teddy was fifty-seven and had busted his gut to buy
this truck, which he was far from done paying for. Now—
even the cops told him—he was supposed to hire a lawyer
to collect from his own insurance company, not his idea
of a good time.

His wife, Leah, said, when he called her, "It's just a big

mistake to think you ever get paid back what you deserve in this world. You're not dead, that's the main thing."

Leah was right—he loved his wife—he'd seen guys spend their best years being pissed off and miserable and very fucking boring about it. So he put himself in debt again to get his rig fixed, to avoid losing more workdays. Which he certainly could not afford. Leah was only working half-time now; they had her daughter, April, finally in some kind of college, and no school after high school was free.

He'd had the truck for five years, and he told everyone he was eager to get back in the saddle, but this was very close to a lie. A large part of him wished he could get away with never driving again. Just when that insane car came at him from nowhere, his mind was on Sally, his ex-wife; he'd been on his way to visit her outside Washington, D.C. And she had such a way of looking at him when he was standing in her doorway, her old look. Could he pay attention to two things at once, why not? And the speediest reflexes couldn't make sixteen tons of unloaded semi move faster than it did—that crappy car had come out nowhere, before any human being could hit any brake. What did he think he could've done? But he kept thinking it. Which was no good to anyone.

He'd called Sally, his ex-wife, from the towing garage—in this rasping, whispering voice that probably sounded like someone else—just to explain where the hell he was, and she was ominously silent at first. Then she said, "Okay, okay. I get it. You're not hurt?"

Sally had a history of being disappointed in him, which caused him to make extra efforts to be dependable now, within their situation. He'd been sleeping with her for a year. They were having a real romance, a separate road from the rest of his life, which was his real life. It wasn't even that complicated. He saw Sally when he was driving anywhere near her, hauling cookies to Florida or cough syrup to Baltimore, and he came home to Leah happy to see her.

He'd married Sally when they were both in their twenties and they hadn't even stayed married that long. She'd hated his being away so much; she was always in a rage by the time he came home. When you were young it wasn't natural to be patient.

He'd met Leah (she liked to call herself his last wife) when they were both older, glad enough to have whatever they could have. He'd helped raise April, the biggest pain in the ass on earth and the most amazing creature. She was eight when he moved in, and she was big on pranks like putting dog kibble in his cereal bowl or dropping grapes into his empty boots. He'd roar in high outrage while she giggled; he liked her tricky spirit.

When he got himself home to Leah after the accident, he must've looked three hundred years old. He'd left the truck outside Baltimore and gotten on a Greyhound to New York (seats not made for his height), and then waited around for another bus to take him to their upstate town,

at the southern edge of the Catskills. He'd spent hours
of the ride making phone calls to try to cover his ass on
runs he couldn't make now. He got a friend to do just one,
and he had to explain to the broker, who was pissed off.
When Leah picked him up at the stop, she said, "Well,
thank God you're in one piece." The God part was a fig-
ure of speech; she wasn't religious. He secretly sort of was,
from so many years trying to lean on a higher power.

He had to wonder if the least he could do after the crash
was to stop seeing Sally. But Sally lived near Washington,
and the truck was in a repair shop a mere hour from her
house. They'd take their time fixing it, earning their enor-
mous estimate, but he'd have to go get it.

The big revival with Sally had begun when she was di-
vorcing a more recent husband and she wanted a copy of
the old divorce agreement with Teddy, which she couldn't
find, did he have it? An email came to him out of the blue
with this question. He hadn't seen her for decades, what
was she up to? She said she'd worked for years as a bookkeeper and now she did something better in IT. Teddy
had only started drinking at the end of their marriage,
but after he got himself into AA, she was on his list of
people he'd caused harm and had to make amends to. He
sent her a letter, saying how sorry he was: for always telling other people how fucked-up she was, for throwing her
nice cocktail dress under his truck and running it over. He
thought she had a few things to be sorry for herself, but
that was not the point. Not at all. She wrote back a not
very respectful note, saying she hoped his new life was a

shitload better than his last, there was a lot of room for improvement, and the next time he heard from her was twenty-six years later.

He still thought of her as young, though she was close to his age. He emailed a picture of himself, a selfie he took by a lake in Michigan, a graying dude who still had most of his hair, and so she sent one of herself—how could someone who'd turned into her own mother still look exactly like Sally? It was humbling to see; she was his first great love.

So when they finally met again, they were prepared. She had a house with a driveway big enough for his truck. No kids at home anymore. She served him coffee in the living room, but they both knew where they were heading. How startling it was to be in that suburban bedroom, figuring out her body all over again. "You were always fast at getting a bra off," she said. She'd learned a lot of moves since they were first married. He knew her and he didn't know her at all.

In the days right after the accident, when he was home all the time, Leah kept saying, "Rest, will you just rest?" as if he were convalescing, as she called it. He was still seeing blood, all the time, slick red all over the car seats, but he didn't have to go on about it. He told Leah he could sleep when he was dead, and he started work on the back porch steps, which he'd been meaning to get to for months. The good news was that the passenger in the Taurus—the man he'd tried to lift out—had survived and was in a hospital getting his broken bones fixed. Teddy thought about going down to Maryland to pay him a visit, but the lawyer said he shouldn't.

April, who now had a summer job in a knitting shop on Main Street, said to him, "Why did he do that, the driver who hit you? Was he stoned?"

April knew about stoned. Her high school in its countryish setting had been a hotbed of who knew what—amphetamines, heroin, synthetic marijuana, and stuff Teddy didn't even recognize by its nicknames—and April's adventuring attitude had led her into deep stupidity and danger from age sixteen on. She'd shift back and forth, walk around all stringy and snarling, then pop up as a perky, shiny-haired teenager; they couldn't keep track, they had no hold on her. She laughed when Teddy offered to take her to an NA meeting. She cut school (which she'd always liked), she stole from her mother's purse (she'd once been overattached to Leah); the usual. It was as if the drugs taught her to mock any ties as false. What held the world together was a bunch of lame assumptions.

She had a big scar slashing across her cheek now from where she'd fallen down the hill of their street when she was high. The surprise of this defacement had had an effect. Teddy had been away for that, but when he got back she was going to a rehab place in Kingston every day. She talked to Teddy now—they were buddies again—so he knew there had been one slip, but his guess was she'd be okay. In the fall she was going to a community college nearby.

Anyway, the kid who'd hit his truck had not been under

the influence of anything. Teddy's lawyer kept him more informed than he even wanted. "He must've just thought he could zip around as fast as he goddamned felt like," Teddy said.

"It's ego, isn't it?" April said. "When people do that."

Good group, that rehab.

"It killed him," she said.

Teddy almost said, *Gets us all, that's always what's the matter*, but he didn't, because he wanted April to be better than that. His girl.

"They should pay you," she said.

Leah, who was glad to have him home so much, got him to help with the gardening. He complained that his back wasn't made for weeding—what was she doing to him?—but he stuck with it. The sun wasn't that hot; it was nice being out in the yard. In the end they got into a little contest pelting each other with blackberries. Her aim was really very good, but when he picked up a green tomato, to escalate, she stopped him. "You know what they cost at the farm stand? I save us a fortune by having this garden, you have no idea."

Everyone likes a cheap tomato, but he was sorry she'd mentioned cash. It was six months since her job had cut back her hours (in the billing office of a hospital—weren't people still getting sick?). The two of them were carrying too much debt, which made Teddy angry again at the asshole who'd careened into his truck.

"Oh, please," Leah said. "Like you never did anything stupid at that age."

They were having this discussion while eating their blackberries with sugar on the porch. It was true that even Leah, the most sensible of women, had done stupid things in her relative youth. She'd fallen asleep drunk and set her bed on fire with a lit cigarette. She'd hitched to Montreal alone in the middle of the night and talked her way out of dirty situations.

"He paid a bigger price than I ever did," Leah said. "That kid."

Leah was right, of course, that what Teddy was complaining about was *only money*. "I bet he was in a rush to get to some girl," Teddy said. He didn't want to imagine too much, actually.

"Or some guy," Leah said. "It's a bigger world now, you know."

I hope he's getting laid in heaven, Teddy almost said. He believed it was petty to picture heaven as a place, but who could help doing it? He'd heard that Muslims had a heaven of endless pleasure and beautiful sex with perfect mates. Teddy did not usually pray for dead people (what good was that?), but he would've sent that crazy, dead driver something good if he could have. Because he was young, especially. Young forever.

Leah got up and went back out to the garden, where she began sweeping leaves off the path. She took impeccable care of the house. It was a fifties house, boxy and small, and she'd had it before she met him, but it had been both of theirs for a long time now. Teddy had just replaced a lot of shingles on the roof in the spring; if rain came in again they were in trouble. He loved this house; he loved coming home to it.

When Teddy went to pick up the truck, he got his friend Jackson to drive him down. Jackson was in on the Sally story. He said, "Everybody has a fling now and then."

They did? Jackson had not, and he said Teddy had all the luck. Jackson didn't know Sally was actually older than Leah. But for Teddy the past made all the fooling around with Sally a young episode; it just worked that way.

The trip took more than five hours, with breaks for food and coffee, and Jackson was a good friend to do it. He wouldn't even let Teddy pay for gas. And he didn't pull out of the repair shop until it was totally clear that the truck was ready. He wasn't going to strand Teddy in the middle of fucking Maryland. When he waved goodbye out the window, he yelled, "Be good, and if you can't be good, be careful," as if it were 1952.

Teddy contemplated this advice as he pulled into Sally's driveway. He would've looked better in Jackson's Subaru, but the truck (with its bolted and soldered patches, its expensively restored brake lines) was his truck. He could see the shape of Sally moving behind the big bay window. He was tired from the drive, and it did occur to him, not for

the first time, that he was sort of a failure in life, to someone like Sally. It was true that on the way to getting ahead
he'd had a tendency to fall on his face. But he was rich
in many things—love and happiness, the most important
things—if he wasn't fucking them up at the moment.

Sally gave him that look when she opened the door; she
looked tickled and hungry and amused at herself. "Hey,
pardner," she said, an old joke of theirs. Teddy acted as
he did every time—he gave her a long hug and a thorough
kiss—but he was not exactly with her. He was a man out
to lunch somewhere.

She might have picked up on this. She led him back to
the kitchen and took a pitcher of iced tea out of the fridge.
"How can you look so tuckered out from someone else
driving?" she said.

Teddy went on about how happy he was to have his rig
back; he'd secretly been afraid they'd find something else
that would cost too much to fix.

Sally, who had her own life, said, "I had a week at work
I wouldn't wish on a dog."

"A dog wouldn't be so great with a computer," Teddy
said. "He'd eat the keyboard."

Sally said her boss was making her organize this year's
staff retreat, oh, God. A retreat, now that Teddy asked,
was when employees had to go off to a hotel in the country
to discuss their vision. She made a puking gesture, finger
down gullet, that April would've used.

"I guess truckers don't have these," Teddy said. "We're
more informal about discussing our visions."

"You have them?"

"We do, and I'm not at liberty to reveal them."

Your basic trucker-philosopher lived in solitude and had too much time to think, too many theories. Teddy was very aware that he was lucky to be married. He liked the alternation of days on the road without a soul to talk to and then time at home with his family all over him. The on-off routine suited someone like him. The season when he'd first met Leah, he'd been alone too long; he was clenched and shy.

And now look. Sally had decided this was enough talk, and she'd gotten up from the table to lead him to the bedroom upstairs. The bed was always tightly made—could bounce a dime off the blanket—and on the dresser was a vase of flowers, waiting for him. Waiting for her, really (what did he care about roses?); she wanted some Valentine sweetness in this.

Teddy could see already that he didn't exactly want to be here. But it would be a cruel moment to turn back— he had no interest in being mean to Sally—and maybe he wanted to be here enough to stay. Apparently he did. It wasn't the best sex they'd ever had, but he did his part, the spirit of the thing took over, they managed fine.

Afterward, when they were lying in the nice cool air-conditioned room, the sweat drying off them, Sally said, "It's no fucking different than it ever was. I still have to wait for you to show up in the truck. Wait all over again."

He hadn't seen this coming. How aggravated her voice was.

"I think it's better if we don't do this anymore," she said. "I've kind of had it. Okay?"

"You sure?" he said.

"Sure enough."

It came to him as bad news, even if it was all for the best. "Okay," he said. "Okay, if you're sure." She was still very pretty. He put his hand on her hip; he wasn't getting up right this instant even though he was going soon. "All right then," he said. He didn't even like her entirely, not the way she was now and maybe not even then, but he wanted a minute for remembering that it had been a great thing to be young with her.

They both fell asleep—like a peaceful couple—before he got up and showered and got himself ready to leave. Outside the windows there was a fading sky with a white moon already showing. He was hungry too, but dinner with Sally was a distinctly poor idea. He wasn't ever going to see her again, was he?

"You be careful when you're driving," she said at the door. "Don't get into any more accidents."

"Wasn't my fault."

"That's what they all say," she said, with a mild chuckle.

"I'll be careful," he said, as if he were answering Jackson.

•

He was really very hungry and he wasn't going to take the truck wandering around Sally's town or onto the clogged streets of Washington. He headed back onto I-95, where there was a rest stop if you went south. Darkness had fallen, and the rest area had a neon glow, the brightness of a roadside settlement of snack bars and gas stations. What a joy and relief it was to sit down in a Formica booth and tank up on a double cheeseburger, fries, apple pie a la mode. He ate as if he'd been running hard all day.

He'd planned to stay over at Sally's, and now he could drive through the night to get home to Leah. But by the time he finished the pie he was thinking a takeoff at dawn made more sense; his semi was a sleeper, with a mattress tucked in the back of the cab, and he could settle for the night right here. Which was what Leah thought he was doing, in fact.

He sent Leah a text—*truck fine miss u like alwys april too all my lv*—and none of it was a lie. There were burning truths in that message.

He couldn't stay in the restaurant booth forever so he went out into what was turning into a very nice summer night, clear and soft. He sat on a bench at the edge of the parking lot, with bushes at the border and the traffic roaring farther down. The accident had happened not too far from here, hadn't it? In fact the driver had probably been exiting from here, while Teddy rolled on below.

April had friends who said they believed in ghosts, and Teddy scoffed at them. But he wished the dead boy could know that the truck was all fixed up and he the driver was perfectly fine. *Don't worry*, he wanted to say to the boy, since you always heard ghosts were restless. *Have a good time in heaven, don't bother resting in peace. We're done, no unfinished business*, as if they could shake hands across the Great Divide.

Above the highway the moon, almost full, was floating in the dark night, with no stars visible. Teddy was thinking about Sally and about how a life as long as his (which wasn't even that long) contained so much old time, great hoards of it filling out the spaces in his head; he didn't feel his younger days as lost exactly. Except that now he'd lost Sally, the later Sally; he did feel that. Too bad for him, that was the way it was, he'd be glad eventually, but he wasn't now.

He didn't sleep very well in the truck, but when his phone alarm woke him at five thirty, he could see the rosy pink of the waking sky, which looked good anywhere. He got cleaned up in the rest area, drank a coffee from a machine since no food place was open, and texted Leah to say he'd be home before lunch. And when he had his foot on the brake at the entry ramp, staying slow to gauge when to merge with traffic, he thought, *There's no justice in who dies, where did I get my luck from?* and then he was on the highway with everybody else.

When he got home, everybody was having a big fat Sunday brunch. The sun was getting hotter, but they were on the screened back porch with fans around them. At the table were April and her friend, Nellie; Leah's friend,

Barbara; and Leah, who'd cooked the stuff—before them were decimated plates of bacon and pancakes and blackberries and whipped cream. "Plenty left for you," Leah said.

He wasn't quite ready for all these people. Nellie, April's friend, said, "Do you think Washington, D.C., would be a good place to live?"

April snorted. "He doesn't notice that," she said. "He just drives."

Before Teddy went on the road the next week, his lawyer had a little news for him over the phone. The payment was always slower for property damage than for injuries. Had he noticed any delayed symptoms—headaches, seizures, seeing double, bouts of dizziness? Sometimes these took a while to appear. Teddy was thinking what a sleaze the lawyer was. Jackson, straight as an arrow himself, had recommended him. Money made everybody want to be so smart. "I have chronic indigestion from paying a fortune for my truck," Teddy said. All the fake whining would be a lost cause; he was healthy as a horse.

The lawyer, who had been paid a retainer, was looking into it further. Teddy wasn't eager to pay him more. He had to pay the bank for his repairs loan, he had to keep paying his truck insurance, he had to keep paying off the truck, he helped Leah with the mortgage, and they got hit for April's tuition before the summer even ended. He had plenty of work, at least—no slowdown from contractors this year—he was on the road as much as he could stand. But he had the sloppy feeling he was waiting for his ship to come in. This was always a chump's position.

April asked him, "Did you ever almost die?"

Teddy thought she'd heard too many war stories from old junkies at her meetings. April herself had straightened up before she bottomed out really thoroughly, so maybe she was a little jealous.

"Not really," Teddy said, "unless you count the time I met Bigfoot when I got out of the truck to pee near Spokane. He wasn't friendly."

"Oh, please."

"I never told you that story?"

"The guy who hit your truck," April said, "do you think he knew what was happening?"

"Yes."

"What do you think he was thinking?"

"Maybe he was asking God for a last-minute break. People try to bargain, we all do."

"God doesn't make deals," April said. "I don't know why people bother with all the repenting and promising."

"I know," Teddy said.

No payment yet from the insurance. He had collision coverage, he knew he did, but there was a high deductible and apparently room for debate on certain issues, according to the lawyer. "Try not to obsess," Leah said.

"How can a person not think about money?" he said. They were having this conversation while walking through a supermarket, buying food for a Thanksgiving dinner. Leah planned to feed eighteen people.

"What if you died the day after tomorrow?" Leah said, throwing two quarts of heavy cream into the cart. "Would you want your mourners to talk about what a skimpy meal they had at your house?" She was throwing two pounds of butter in too.

Teddy was living in two worlds, a tidy house overflowing with abundance and behind the walls a hidden boneyard of bills and strained credit. "Everybody lives that way," Leah said. Not much of a defense.

And right on Thanksgiving an email from Sally appeared on his phone. *Maybe I've been too hard on you,* she wrote. First time he'd heard that from her. *The truck is your livelihood. You're a hardworking person.* This was a lot of crap, but the point was that she wouldn't shut the door on him if he happened to be driving south any time. If he was still interested.

Teddy didn't answer, but all through Thanksgiving dinner he was a man overstuffed with tempting offers, a man who had more opportunities than he could begin to swallow. The masses of food on the table made sense to him; he laughed at the clutter of sweet potatoes, white potatoes, Brussels sprouts, creamed onions, corn pudding, green bean casserole, white meat, dark meat, stuffing, two kinds of cranberry sauce. That was the beauty of it. "*Dad*," April said. "Will you stop putting gravy all over my plate?"

"Everybody, eat," he said. "No leftovers!"

He didn't answer Sally right away, he'd get to it when he knew what he wanted to say. He was thinking about the time he ran over her little fancy black dress. He'd been so angry at the dress, which was hanging on the closet door, ready for her to put on when she went out with her friends. He hated the way she was with her friends, hyped-up and full of herself and showing off to any men. She was screaming at him when he grabbed the dress and dashed out the door to throw it down in the driveway. "You asshole fucking loser," she screamed. But she stayed away from the moving truck; she was afraid of the truck. He couldn't remember being a person like that. Yes, he could.

After he wrote her the ninth-step letter of apology, someone at a meeting said that he should've replaced the dress, sent a new one. But who wanted an item of clothing from an ex-husband? And a check would have been insulting in another way. Somebody said a gift certificate (a what?). He'd assumed his genuine remorse was enough—it was a lot, from him—but how much of life was weighable and concrete and physical and how much was the-thought-that-counted? He was still figuring that one out.

On the other hand, maybe he understood it as far as he needed, since he wasn't about to see Sally in person again. He'd decided that, despite all the haunting she did of his mind. Why be a jerk if you didn't have to be? The logic of this was strong in him when he finally wrote. And probably she was already mad from waiting too long for him to answer. She hated waiting.

It was February before the lawyer let him know that the money from the insurance company had come through at last. "It may not be what you hoped for," the lawyer said, "but I don't feel you have grounds to be disappointed." So it wasn't anywhere near what it should've been but it was something. Teddy could put the check in the bank and pay off some of his debt. Some.

"They're sharks," April said. "They don't care about us. Your lawyer too, he's a shark."

Leah was surprised that anything had been paid at all. "Reason to celebrate," she said. Teddy said he wasn't going out for any big dinners with clinked glasses. He just wanted to not think about it anymore. Was that too much to ask? He just wanted to drive his rig.

"Right you are," Leah said. "It's done. Over and done."

Two months after he'd written Sally his definite decision, he found himself with a load of soup cans heading south on I-95, not far from her neck of the woods. He wasn't going there; he didn't have to go there. But he did stop at the rest area outside Baltimore, which was really one of the better rest stops. How familiar it was now, the signs and the stores and the now-spindly borders of bushes.

It was midafternoon, a bleak winter day. He needed coffee, he needed a piss and a break from the highway, and he was pleased to sit in the café, taking his time over a donut. He stayed at the counter close to an hour, stalling before he got back on the road; he seemed to think of this highway entrance as a devil's pass.

April had those questions about whether he'd ever almost died. Of course he had, during certain years of his life. Once when he took a beautiful drunken walk across a frozen pond and midway the ice cracked and broke. Once when he was in a car with a woman who drove them off the road into a gully. Once when he was in a fight with a guy who was crazier than he seemed. He'd had a good time when he was young, but in certain respects youth was overrated.

Okay, he had to get back in his truck now, no matter what, and he got up and made his way across the cold parking lot. Inside the truck, he sat again, looking out through the windshield. Nobody had forced him to stop at this stop. He missed Sally, the pang was worse here, her voice was in his head, more than her voice. He was never going to see her again, and that was the way it was.

Teddy was a good driver, nobody said he wasn't, and when he got the engine started and had the rig out of the parking area, he moved very slowly, looked all the ways he had to look, slipped onto the ramp and waited as long as he had to before he rolled into traffic, thinking all the time of the unlucky boy driving that crapmobile car, rushing to get to some girl.

5

One thing Kiki knew—her niece was having some sort of trouble with the boyfriend. There was no reason for her to stay at Kiki's apartment on some bullshit excuse about a playground—was it to get away from him? And at their last lunch, Reyna had been in such a hurry to answer his text, as if it didn't pay to make him wait. Not a good sign.

Kiki knew the risks of lecturing her niece, giving too much direct advice, but maybe this was the time. And Reyna had long pestered her with questions about Osman and the invisible years of marriage in Turkey—was that her way of trying for guidance? Kiki had always made a point of not speaking against Osman (she was less sour about marriage than Reyna's parents), which confused Reyna. "What was wrong with him? You never tell me," Reyna said, "why you left."

•

The best time with Osman had been the years in Istanbul. Most majestic of cities—she used to stand at the window at dusk to watch crowds of gulls swooping in arcs around the spires and minarets. Dusk in winter was when she waited for Osman to come home, listened for footsteps in the street below. But smitten though she was—rightly smitten—she had never expected it to last.

Was that Osman's doing? Had he been the older, more serious one? What had he seen in her? He liked her right away, too; they talked three hours that first afternoon, and he'd said how "unusual" she was, in a tone that was extremely sexy at the time.

By now she'd spent a lifetime congratulating herself on choosing Turkey, but it had been a random choice, a place she wandered into off the ferry from Greece. *The meeting point of East and West*, she wrote to her family. What she intended to say was that it had a strangeness Europe didn't have, codes she couldn't guess at but was sure she was learning.

In the old days she and her friend Pat used to walk by the city walls—the old Theodosian Walls—and see gypsy women forage for leafy plants that grew in the dirt near the ancient lines of stones. Greens for cooking. Pat told her you could see that still.

And now everyone was developing a bad opinion of Turkey. The news was full of Istanbul lately, protests against a government plan to destroy a park near Taksim to build a fake-historic shopping mall. Kiki's TV showed policemen moving in on crowds, using water cannons and tear gas, setting fire to demonstrators' tents. The coverage went from being jolly, with protestors dancing in lines and waving clever signs, to being horrific, with people shrieking as they fled.

It was too familiar. In the years with Osman, Kiki had written home to her family that the "civic unrest" they were reading about wasn't really so bad—lots of countries had labor strikes and student riots, nothing special about Istanbul. She really was against worrying; it took a few years before the street actions turned rougher, more chaotic—bombs went off in cafés; snipers fired from rooftops at workers' demonstrations. Death squads from the right-wing Grey Wolves raided the apartments of leftists to murder them; factions on the left began to favor armed revolt. Kiki refused to be frightened away, but plenty of foreigners were. Nobody was idly wandering into Osman's shop; his rugs went unbought. There was no need to explain this in her letters, which took forever to get home anyway.

Osman had opinions—pro-labor ones—but he wasn't ever a participant. How could anyone believe in assassinations? Some of his friends sort of did; they had long discussions into the night that Kiki could not quite follow.

She should've tried harder to follow. She always knew more about what Empress Theodora said to Justinian in the sixth century than what was happening a neighborhood away. Where did she think she was? In a tender bower watched over by her Turkish protector? In a guarded harem gossiping with Pat? But her love for the city had been genuine.

Pat still looked the same to Kiki, and how was that possible? More pinched and creased, but not so different—sandy hair cut short in tufts, pert alert face, scratchy voice. She came to the States almost every year and each time Kiki exclaimed at her sameness.

In their very young days in Istanbul, they used to say, "I could never go back, could you?" And Pat had stayed. She had a great apartment, north of Taksim, big and rambling, with casement windows and a terrace that flowed with ivy, leftover from a husband she hadn't had for twenty years. She had two kids, now grown. Kiki had seen photos of all of them, looming out of emails or sent as snapshots in the folds of letters. She still had one of Pat's son at maybe nine, a boy warrior in a satin costume with a sequined cape and feather-tipped headgear, all dressed up for his circumcision ceremony. They were really Turkish, Kiki thought. Pat had a whole Turkish life.

On every visit back, Pat said Istanbul was different now, more spruced up and modern, not as clogged with ruined buildings. Every year Pat invited her to come to Turkey again, and every year Kiki said sometime she would.

And now Osman had started writing to her, sending emails out of the blue. A man whose voice she hadn't heard in thirty-odd years. He looked older in his photos but still Osman. After all this time she must be indistinct information to him, a jumble of phrases in his past, silliness in English, radiance in bed. Not entirely remembered but never gone. It was one of the mysteries of modern life, what happened to old love.

Kiki was picturing Pat's street, the rows of old Ottoman buildings with their windowed rooms jutting out from the upper floors. She might have had Pat's life. Kiki thought that now whenever they saw each other. She might've stayed in Turkey forever, if she and Osman hadn't moved to the farm.

It was a small, slightly ramshackle farm, and at first she'd been so proud of herself, to see where love was bringing her next. A girl from Brooklyn feeding the chickens and the geese—taken into something she knew nothing about, the elements of a very old way. The countryside around the farm looked like desert half the year, but it was rich volcanic soil, green after the snowmelt. Osman's aunt taught her to help with the barn work and the kitchen work and the washing. Kiki didn't mind the nonsmelly parts of the work, but some of it was awful (killing the chickens, for instance) and there was too much of it, over and over, and Osman had spells of being demoralized about the move, which made him look different to her.

She hadn't expected to be lonely there. She thought of herself as someone who liked her own company, who'd grown out of the habit of idle social talk. But farm work was not that kind of solitude. They still scolded her about the mistakes she'd made at first. Each task required attention, and the day was one task after another.

The winters were the worst—when kitchen work started before daylight and snow fell for days and the house was never warm enough. Even the roosters, who crowed through the night, sounded full of petulance. But she might have stayed for years, winter summer winter, if not for the antiquities. (Had she really called them that? She had. Savoring the academic sound of it.) She had known what they were, better than the others, and had wanted to look at them, to hold them.

The three Germans arrived in the summer of 1977. Two men, Bruno and Dieter, and Bruno's girlfriend, Steffi. They were passing through the region in a Volkswagen van, and they stopped on the road to look at the fruit trees. Kiki came out to tell them they could pick the peaches (which they were about to do anyway)—she was very excited to see foreigners. The farm was at the southern edge of Cappadocia where tourists never came. Kiki spoke to them in Turkish and then in English—they all had very good English.

Over her jeans the girl wore a long T-shirt she'd knotted at her hip. *I could do that*, Kiki thought, as if there were any reason to be stylish here. "You are a person living in the house?" Bruno said. He was the bigger, blonder one.

When Kiki invited them to supper, her aunt-in-law didn't grumble—she was too curious—and Osman's father and Osman went upstairs and got themselves cleaned up better than usual for the meal.

Bruno said, "This is the eggplant the best in Turkey."

"I think you live well," Dieter said. He was admiring the kilim under the table, a red-and-black beauty from Konya with geometric motifs.

"I used to sell these," Osman said. "I wasn't clever enough so I had to go live where no one is clever." How bitter he sounded, her poor husband.

His father, who understood a little, said, "Osman had very, very good carpets," and Kiki translated.

"We are selling things but we don't have a shop," Steffi said.

Osman's father brought out the bottle of *rakı*, and even Aunt Ayşe had a few snorts. Ayşe was having a high old time, asking the guests if they knew any songs. To Kiki's surprise, Dieter sang, not badly, "I Want to Hold Your Hand." *Komm, gib mir deine Hand!* He had wire-rimmed glasses, like John Lennon's, and a really nice voice. On the last verse he held his hand out to Kiki. By then it was dark outside, they'd lit the lanterns on the table, and Osman's father refused to let the guests think of driving anywhere now. No, they didn't have bandits anymore but sometimes on the roads they had people like them.

After the old folks went to bed, Osman, who'd learned some of his English from rock records, took it upon himself to sing the Beatles songs he knew. He went through all the verses to "Michelle" and "Rocky Raccoon." *Michelle, my belle.* What a good mimic he was—he sounded like Paul, he sounded like John! Kiki laughed so hard she practically wet herself. He was usually in bed by this hour.

They agreed that Beatles songs sounded old to them
now, but what did "old" mean? Osman, who posed this
question, had sort of fallen asleep in his chair by the time
Steffi went out to the van to bring back her illustration
of what old meant. She came in with a duffel the size of
a boulder, and beneath its zipper, wrapped in two blan-
kets tied with string, was a big clay bottle—an amphora.
Pale dry terra-cotta, with a fat curved middle and a long
neck and two handles with designs incised in them and
a pointed bottom where it had once been sunk in sand
while stored on a Greek ship. It was a utilitarian object,
meant to be smashed after use, but Kiki gasped when
Steffi stroked the surface. It was probably two thousand
years old. "Around that," Steffi said.

Of course, it could be a fake. The Germans weren't ex-
perts, only self-informed crooks. And amphorae weren't all
that rare anyway. It wasn't even so valuable. But Kiki lost
her breath looking at it. It was right *there*. The Germans
were so amused by her response that they brought out another one—more battered, with a piece chipped off the
spout and sea growth encrusted on one side.

Osman woke while she was getting her nerve up to
touch it. She heard him say in Turkish, "What's this?" and
she told him. Everyone went quiet while Osman sat taking
in the whole scene.

Bruno took the moment to reach into his jacket pocket
and show off his sack of gold Byzantine coins. He put
one in Kiki's hand—the size of a nickel, thin as a dime—
and she looked at an emperor's head, drawn as roughly

as a cartoon, and tried to make out the letters around it, D N IVSTINI I. Could it mean Justinian the First? It could.

"You must put this back in the car before you sleep," Osman said. "Please not to leave them in my house." He got up and left the room then, without any goodnights.

"Too much *rakı*, it's late," Kiki said. "Hey. Could I see a few more coins before we all go to bed?"

"She loves this. I knew she would be loving this," Bruno said.

Dieter said, "She has the mind for it."

What a mishmash of things they had. The Seljuk tiles were the most beautiful—turquoise glaze with black calligraphy. Thirteenth-century, if real. Did they just buy whatever anyone offered at a low price? Apparently.

"It's hard we don't speak Turkish," Dieter said. "Better we have someone who speaks Turkish."

"Maybe you can come to have a little vacation with us," Steffi said.

"Not too long," Dieter said, "unless you want long." He wasn't bad-looking either, with brown thick hair brushed back, steady eyes.

Kiki was astonished. She didn't even know these people. Was this her next adventure, come in off the road to summon her? Bruno was saying something in German to the others. Steffi said, "In the morning we can talk." Kiki went to get all the bedding for them from the cupboards, and she noticed that she was feeling high on the whole idea.

When she went in to Osman, he wasn't even asleep.

"You can stay up later with your friends," he said, from the bed. "I know you want to."

"No, no," she said.

She settled next to him. He hadn't taken a full bath before dinner, and a trace of barn smell (which she had once liked) clung to his skin when she was close to him. How hard he worked, a man with a serious life. The Germans seemed younger. Crime, of course, was serious, but they didn't act as if it was. They were in it for the sport of it, the travel opportunities.

She and Osman lay in bed in a cold silence, until she heard him breathing slowly in sleep. She stayed awake so long she heard the wailing notes of the call to prayer two hours before dawn. Osman and his father didn't go to mosques very often—his father was an old-style fan of Atatürk, anti-clerical—but Aunt Ayşe had a sweet sort of piety. Kiki dressed covered up when she went into the village, but people left her alone, to be who she was. Who was she?

Was she someone who could take off, just like that, on a reckless and interesting escapade? She saw herself shifting into a new life in Europe as a Turkish history expert, a sexy outlaw. What had ever made her think she could be a farm wife? It fit with a romance about wanting to live more deeply, and not all of that was silly. Most of what she'd known before had seemed brittle and trivial, when she first came to the farm.

For a hardheaded person, she had let herself be flung about by the winds of love, and she wasn't sorry either.

Was love her religion? What a devoted practitioner she was. If there were no Osman, there would have to be someone else. Was the Dieter guy offering himself as a candidate? Kiki had some pleasant moments imagining him as a lover—he would be confident, unrelenting, generous—very, very taken with her. Maybe Germany was a great place to live. Could a Jew ever go to Berlin as if it were just anywhere? People did now. It was too weird to have these thoughts while lying next to Osman, but what did that tell you?

When Kiki woke the next day—in time, which was a miracle, to make breakfast for Osman and his father—her first thought was to hope the Germans had moved their loot back into the van, as instructed. While Osman slept on, she peeped into the room downstairs where she'd settled them on pillows, and in the early light she could see the two red-clay amphorae, still unwrapped, near their piles of clothes. If Steffi rolled too far in her sleep, she could smack right into them.

It made Kiki angry—none of what they smuggled was especially precious to these people. And where would the pieces end up? On some burgher's bookshelf, five thousand miles from here. Osman was right to be horrified.

Kiki got a fire going in the kitchen hearth, and she reheated the barley and warmed the leftover bread and started the coffee, so Osman and his father would smell it and come down, which they did.

Osman's father said, "They are dreaming of their digestions, our guests."

"How many more days will they sleep?" Osman said.

The men were off working in the fields and Kiki was in the chicken coop when the Germans finally got up. She could hear them trying to talk to Aunt Ayşe in the kitchen. They were all happily eating peaches when Kiki came in. Dieter was drawing preposterous pictures to show where Germany was, and Aunt Ayşe was giggling behind her hand.

When Osman and his father came back for the midday meal, several hours later, all of them were shrieking with laughter over Bruno's imitation of the chickens in the yard. Bruno had a clownish side. Steffi was wearing an apron—the lentil soup was ready; the stewed purslane was ready. "Chow time," Kiki said, a phrase only Osman understood. Osman sat without saying a word. Kiki sputtered with hilarity when Steffi said, "Right now in Berlin I would eat pickled herring to cure this hangover. Really, it cures." Let Osman glower; Kiki could laugh if she wanted.

The men were back in the field when Kiki helped the Germans pack up their van. She made sure the amphora duffels were wedged securely between the valises. "See, you are so careful, you should come," Dieter said. Steffi wrote down the name of a hotel in Ankara. "You can find us in this place in a week, if you decide like that." Had Kiki ever said she was deciding? Dieter gave her a souvenir, a tarnished Ottoman coin from 1903, with the old Arabic script on it. "Not so valuable," he said, looking into her eyes. "Only good to look at." Kiki still had it, a token from an unled life.

"You had fun with your new friends, I know," Osman said, in their room that night. He said it sourly, and no protests satisfied him, no avowals. She loved him (she argued), she wasn't going anywhere, did she have to swear to him? It didn't matter what Kiki said. He'd seen her, falling all over herself in her excitement at being with these people, and look who they were. "It surprised them," he said, "that someone like you lives here, outside a village smaller than a raisin. I'm sure they think your quaint husband is so simple he believes you'll stay in such a place."

Well. Maybe she didn't want to stay. Maybe she never had. Maybe the whole thing from the start was a very misguided idea and it wasn't her idea either. He'd gotten this scheme in his head all by himself. She couldn't stop saying any of it. This was the beginning of a new phase, unflattering to both.

They seemed to be at a delicate point, where a very strong love was needed to bind them together, habit wasn't enough. They kept trying to reach for what they had once had. Near the end, as a desperate plan, she tried to talk him into moving to America with her. Osman wasn't going to leave his family, who would do a thing like that? Well, she had. And he'd never thought well of her for it either.

She regretted not going off with the Germans when she had the chance. In the farmhouse she and Osman were self-conscious at the very sight of each other, ashamed of their turned feelings. Aunt Ayşe and Osman's father didn't know what to do. His father decided to speak very little.

Ayşe, who was often alone with Kiki in their work, grew impatient and cross—said Kiki was tossing the chickens too much feed or she was sloppy in the way she mopped. Ayşe no longer trusted her.

But the heart of the matter was Osman. Every so often, as Kiki tried to ready herself to leave, she remembered why she had vowed to never give up Osman. Dearest of men, rarest of spirits, what the fuck was she doing? But when they approached each other with sweetness (in speech or in bed) the gestures were thin and artificial. One part of the truth was smothering what they had left.

When Kiki left the farm, she took a bus all the way to Istanbul. She was going backward in time. It was a long ride, in late November, chilly the whole way, and she had plenty of time to look out the window—to see the conical Seljuk towers, the leftover Ottoman mosques, the tufa caves and "fairy chimneys" tourists came for—and to think: had she always despised Turkey? There were wonderful things out the window, and she despised them all; they had become a landscape that opposed her, that hulked as further evidence nothing here was for her.

In Ankara, she had to change to another bus, and till it arrived she sat on a bench with her belongings piled around her so that no one stole them. One man kept saying, "You are from America? *Ingiltere? Almanya?* Tell me!" and a younger one kept asking if she needed a husband. They weren't dangerous but she hated them.

Istanbul would at least be better. How grandiose Osman
had been, in his purist way, to drag them off to that farm.
What a fraud she had been to agree to it. Had she ever
believed herself? She had. In Istanbul she could go back to
what she was. She wouldn't have Osman in her way.

She was elated when the bus pulled into the city, her
city, with its stately boulevards and slumped old houses.
On a sloped hill of a street she stayed with Pat, who had
her husband and the first of her kids then. Kiki slept in the
room with the three-year-old, a lively girl who wasn't the
best sleeper. She had almost no money. Osman had made
a point of giving her as many bills as he could spare, but
they didn't add up to much.

On the bus she'd carried, stashed above the seat, three
rugs leftover from the store. They always folded smaller
than you thought. Osman had wanted her to have these, a
legacy, something for whatever home she had someday. He
brought them up from the storeroom with great ceremony,
long hugs, real kisses.

Now they were under her cot in this room she shared
with Pat's little girl. She'd find work; she knew how to
work. She'd get money. Through the night, waking and
sleeping in bursts, Kiki understood all over again that she
really had lost Osman—another version of their fate had
stopped being imaginable—and the tooth of regret tore at
her heart, though she couldn't have said what she regretted or what she would undo.

At breakfast, Pat's husband, Halil, teased her about being a farmwife and told his daughter that Kiki had pulled

a plough all by herself, just like an ox, which the kid believed. Kiki didn't mind Halil—a bit of a blowhard at times but he could be fun. "You came back on purpose to this city where we kill each other for politics?" Halil said.

Pat said, "Please, she just got here. She's getting her bearings."

"Maybe you'll go to Israel," Halil said. "Thousands of people doing that now."

He wasn't ill-natured but he never forgot that she was Jewish. "How did I not remember what it's like here?" Kiki said.

He thought she meant the politics. "Tel Aviv more peaceful," he said. "For you."

It was a rainy and chilly season in Istanbul; the fall mists were turning to winter sleet. She couldn't stay at Pat's forever—as even Pat began to hint by Christmas—and she got work finally as a night clerk in a hotel, a lonely job that came with its own dismal room but barely a salary. Her allotted room was an underheated chamber in the hotel's basement. She was not supposed to bring men there, and she didn't.

By the end of that long winter, Kiki had sold two of the rugs. She had to eat, didn't she? The first two went for cash to live on, but the other one, the best, she kept folded in her suitcase. She had fewer friends left in Istanbul than she'd expected. When the weather wasn't too cold, she went with Pat to the park and they ran around with her rambunctious little daughter. Pat was pregnant again and happy about it.

Walking back to the hotel one damp day, Kiki ran into an American guy that she'd known before—Rob? Was it Rob?—who taught English in a private high school. "You're looking good," he told her. "We should have a drink or something." All at once she was full of hope— maybe this was what she should've done all along, a fellow American. She had many steamy images of their happy future together, before they met in a café the next Monday, which was her one night off. "Can't believe you're here again," he said. He complained about his teaching ("spoiled American brats, sneaky little Turks"), kept saying he hated Istanbul ("you know the cops are controlled by the CIA"), and made fun of the waiter to her ("how would I look with that mustache?"). Nothing could have made her miss Osman more purely and more thoroughly. She was speechless from despair by the time Rob finally said goodnight (startled by her lack of interest) in front of the hotel.

How grim her basement room looked, with its sink in the corner, its mattress on the floor. What was she doing here? She was thirty years old. She wasn't supposed to keep food in the room, but a can of peach nectar, a consoling beverage, was in her satchel. For lack of a can opener, she had to hack at it with a penknife, and she was making good progress, until she saw she'd cut herself with the jagged lid. Why was she bleeding so much? She bled on her best sweater, which she'd worn for her date, and she bled on the hotel's bedspread too. She heard herself shriek and curse, and she moved fast, bandaging her hand with a sock, soaking her sweater in the sink, dabbing at the bedspread with a soapy washcloth. What could they do to her? No one could do anything to her. Fire her, make her pay for the spread? So what. But she was moaning as she worked.

She was remembering when Osman had cut himself like that, doing something with a shovel and a thornbush, and he'd come into the house and bled all over the table-cloth in the kitchen, which she had just washed in a tub with a wringer the day before and had taken off the line that morning. "What is the matter with you?" she said. "You never think for a second about what I have to do. Have you ever fucking washed anything? You never think of anyone but your own ridiculous self." Hate had risen in her and she hadn't seen—how could she not have seen?— that Osman's father was in the kitchen. She had spoken that way to Osman in front of his father (who understood her fine). Osman had a look of shock and rancor, and his father, whom she saw out of the corner of her eye, had horror in his face.

And what had she been doing, yelling at a bleeding man? Why had she hated her husband? Every marriage had that in it. It made her never want to be married. Maybe some marriages were better. She was sorry to have been that person, the hater. She had a long list of things he'd done she hated. Not so long ago either. It was what it was.

And now she'd gotten herself here, to this room like

an urban stable, huddled for the night under a wet bed-spread. All the bedding was sodden now, and just because she would fall asleep anyway didn't mean she was doing so well for herself. Look at how she'd been scrubbing the coverlet, in fear of the manager. His threats, his contempt. She was too old for this crap.

The last rug, the saved one, the most beautiful, would have to go for her ticket home. If she'd hoped to keep it she'd been wrong. In the next week, she walked care-fully through neighborhoods she knew and some she didn't, until she found a dealer she was sure didn't know Osman. In the preliminary chatting he flirted and praised her Turkish, which he claimed was better than his sister spoke. The man was poker-faced when she unfurled the rug—well, that was his job—but when she asked him to name a price, he stunned her. He started with three times what she had guessed, and she bargained him up to more than that. Had Osman known what this thing was worth? It was a Sivas carpet, in good condition for its age (did they have the age wrong?), subtle in its colors, very Persian in its designs. The dealer, a handsome Kurd named Emir, paid her in cash from his safe, as dealers did. She was as-tonished when she walked out the door.

The next day she showed up at the store to buy back the rug. It seemed to her that she had tricked Osman by getting all this money for it. It shouldn't be sold. What else did she have from her marriage, which had been a real marriage? Emir the dealer was not having any of this. When the summer tourists came, he would get much more than he'd just paid for it. Very sorry. He'd already hung it where it could be seen from the street.

This was a low point. She was choked with vain and useless regret. When would she stop making mistakes? The rug dealer was bringing her tea, with his apologies, and a dish of candies. "Eat, please. You're like the beautiful French girls, too thin. Are you French?"

If she flirted back, would he change his mind about the rug? "So all the French girls come to see you?"

"Not me," he said. "My carpets."

But this was enough to get them going. He was easy to talk to, playful but modest (not so usual), and he had a fabulous hawkish face with swooping eyebrows. He'd been in Istanbul only six years, his cousin brought him, he liked music, did she like music, and so on. Yes, she loved music. It was a shock to feel attracted to him—and to find herself, by the next evening, in bed with someone who wasn't Osman. Emir had real gallantry in him, and she was returned to her own body in a way she hadn't even asked for. He was a stroke of luck.

Their hot and good-natured romance lasted much longer than she expected, from late winter until the end of the next summer. At night, before they fell asleep, she liked to murmur, "*S'pas*," into his ear, which meant "thank you" and was the one word he'd taught her in Kurmancî, his dialect of Kurdish. In elementary school he'd been punished for not speaking Turkish. How he'd gotten himself to Istanbul was a long story with so many bypaths she could never follow all of it. He was quite something, she thought.

She always knew she would have to leave, though later she believed he was, if you counted things a certain way, one of the great passions of her life. Still, there was a wife somewhere outside Diyarbakır, a fact he'd slipped into a sentence early on. Kiki pictured her as lumpish and naive but had never asked. It wasn't a good situation, was it? Emir was heartbroken when Kiki left but maybe he was relieved. And he never would sell her back the Sivas carpet, though in the end he loaded her up with newer, cheaper rugs, her dowry for the next stage of her life.

And Pat had been there all this time. She'd had her kids, with and without a husband, and she used to write Kiki tart, sarcastic letters about how divorce with two pre-teens in the house was not as glorious as you might think. (Letters on blue tissue-thin airmail paper, weeks in arriving—what century was that?)

At least Pat still came back to America. Every summer they had their two weeks together at the beach, a custom that had begun when Pat's children were small and needed entertaining. Kiki loved those weeks, the rented cottage with its sagging porch, the long talks by the dunes. What if her ties with Pat hadn't held? Would Turkey have blurred in her mind, gone the way of outdated clothes that looked baffling later, stories whose points were lost?

And now Osman was writing to her. By his own account Osman lived now in a better neighborhood than he ever had, on the leafy outskirts of Istanbul, in a house he said looked like a giant sugar cube. Kiki supposed she was glad he'd done better in the rug business the second time around. He had a son with this wife, a boy who now did something with computers.

Reyna had asked her more than once about money in the marriage, what did they live on? What indeed. A mystery compared to nowadays. Reyna looked upon her aunt as a creature of great hardiness, and Kiki was happy to convey some message about pulling up your socks.

Kiki did tell her stories of how she used to ride a donkey off into the woods to gather kindling, piling the branches before her on its neck. In fact she'd done this just once on a neighbor's donkey, which she hadn't really known how to steer; both families laughed themselves silly.

Let Reyna have that picture of her, her aunt getting herself around by whatever means were at hand, on a braying beastie in the hinterlands. She hadn't fallen off; that was the main thing.

The donkey ride must've been in early winter, when they were stocking up on wood. In winter Kiki had time to read, though it was hard to get books. She could remember trying to explain to Ayşe the plot of a novel—was it *Jane Eyre?*—and how the character had had to decide her fate. She could tell this deciding business made no sense to Ayşe (who got to do that?). And later it was Ayşe who had been the most confused and resentful when Kiki left.

Did Kiki always brag too much about the farm? On Pat's visits in the summertime, when they drove to popular farm stands on the Cape, Kiki was always speaking poorly of the local produce, spurning it forever for not being Turkish. She claimed—and she was almost sure this was true—that the peaches they grew in Cappadocia ripened to a color almost reddish. "They're still better in Turkey, aren't they?" Kiki said. "The vegetables and all the fresh things?"

"Of course," Pat would say. "But don't get sentimental."

Was that a danger?

Even in Turkey she hadn't cried, except at the very end, when Emir was helping to carry her silly assortment of baggage through the airport.

Emir had said, in his steady voice, "You will be fine wherever you go." In the midst of her tears she laughed when he intoned this—it had no way to be true, it was more of a farewell prayer—but she was so happy hearing him say it she came close to not leaving. She didn't *have* to go. But she went.

Once she was back in New York, she needed cash, and she sold as many of his rugs as she could, as soon as she could, keeping just two for herself. One of these she later gave to her niece, when Reyna had a decent place of her own. A Kula carpet, very intricate and beautiful, a golden ground with blue and cream and brown. It vastly improved Reyna's living room. Nomads—Kiki had to tell her—had once invented these tough carpets (Oliver could spill stuff on it) to carry from one seasonal dwelling to another, to warm the hard ground for sleeping and give any tent the mark of home.

6

When Dieter and Bruno and Steffi left the farmhouse on the edge of Cappadocia, they were all getting along well, for a change. Dieter was doing the driving, and despite the glare of the noonday sun bouncing off the windshield, he was in an excellent mood. They'd been dealing with Turks for two months, but they didn't often get inside their houses. How amazing that rough hearth had been, with its blocks of stone and its pit of ash. Dieter felt he would remember that after he forgot everything else. "That was the real Turkey, right there," Bruno said. Dieter was still amazed by the American girl, keeping house with that granny in the middle of nowhere. If they'd stayed longer, he could've gotten her to come with them. He was sure of it.

"Could you be more conceited?" Steffi said.

"She has a husband, this Kiki," Bruno said. "Some people want to stay married forever."

Bruno was unlikely to be such a person—he cheated on anyone he was with, including Steffi, who'd had to wait two days when he disappeared in Istanbul with a very pretty underage Italian. Steffi was not necessarily the patient type either. Lately she'd been giving Dieter the eye. The American girl was lucky she wasn't walking into this.

The drive to Ankara took the rest of the afternoon. Steffi was eager to get near the archaeological digs in that part of Turkey. "You know those workers walk off with bits of loot fresh from the digs," Steffi said. "Everybody wants a few extra lire. They're waiting for us."

Steffi was the best bargainer of them all. She could start so low the seller gasped in shock, she could tease and flirt and get huffy and walk away. Much handshaking and fellowship at the end. The real joy of the trip for her was in those moments. Her face was hardly ever like that, shining.

They got into Ankara a little late for any bargaining in shops. Still, they tried. Near what seemed to be a market square, they went into any stores they found that had old brass bowls in the window or dusty prayer beads. Anything older in the back? No one said yes. No one knew anyone else who might help. Shrugs and headshakes. Bruno's jokes were not getting laughs. A lot of people spoke nothing but Turkish. Maybe you needed names here, maybe you had to know someone.

Too bad they didn't have the American girl with them. She could have figured out what was going on. She could have asked the right questions, with her fast Turkish and her knowing eyes.

The three of them stayed overnight in a faded but endearing hotel near the citadel, with nice old furniture and erratic plumbing. All through dinner, at a café nearby, Dieter was watching to see if Kiki was coming. At least two women on the street could've been her but weren't. He knew it was unlikely she'd get to Ankara so soon, if she decided to come at all, but he was waiting, nonetheless. Steffi said, "Why are you so out of it tonight?"

Hours later, Dieter lay on the bed in his room, under a humming ceiling fan, smoking the last bit of hash from Istanbul and reading a backdated copy of *Der Spiegel* by a dim lamp. He could hear Steffi and Bruno through the wall, laughing and arguing and then sending a rhythm of creaking bedsprings. What was he doing, hearing other people fuck, like a lonely student? He was thirty-three, not so young. (How old was Kiki? He should've asked her.) The smuggling had been his idea, too. For too long he'd been making no money at all as a designer of typeface and clever lettering for advertisements. He'd known Bruno would want to come along—they'd played in the same rock band in college—but Steffi got on his nerves. Maybe he wouldn't see either of them so much, once they were all back in Germany. Once they all had their money. He was getting homesick for Berlin, for his friends, his apartment. Maybe Kiki would visit him in Berlin.

At breakfast the next day, yogurt and olives and bread and tea, Dieter and Steffi had a difference of opinion. Steffi thought they should leave this no-good city at once and take off down the road to where the archaeological digs were, three or four hours away. "You think we'll find a hotel, in the middle of nowhere?" Dieter said. "Don't be crazy. We should go as a day trip and drive back here."

"I'm not crazy. Our lovely van shouldn't be driven more than it has to," Steffi said.

Taking a Volkswagen bus had maybe not been the best idea. Some roads were too narrow for it and too rocky—it wasn't the most stable vehicle in the world. They'd had one breakdown in Bulgaria nobody wanted to think about.

Dieter did want to give Kiki a chance to show up in Ankara, and he began to think he might stay on in the hotel here if the others insisted on leaving. He didn't say this, but he had the idea in his head.

But Bruno voted with him to come back that night—maybe just to spite Steffi. Dieter had a distinct feeling Bruno planned to ditch her once they got back to Germany.

The morning was glaring hot and it was Bruno's turn to drive. In the car he played cassettes they'd brought with them—Nina Hagen, eccentric and loud, was his favorite—so the car became a corner of Berlin, Bruno's corner. A club on wheels. Dieter was startled when he looked through the window and saw road signs in Turkish and a landscape of dry hills with donkeys in the fields.

It wasn't so easy to find any of the archaeological digs either. At a town that was just a row of stores, Bruno's attempt to pantomime shoveling dirt got him nothing by way of directions. They were totally lost on a side road when they stumbled across a cleared area that looked promising. The road forked to a gravel byway and there it was: red dirt and rubble, with roped-off sections like garden plots, where Turkish men dug in room-size pits already deep as their waists. A sign said DEUTSCHES ARCHÄOLOGISCHES INSTITUT, and then in English, GERMAN ARCHAEOLOGI-CAL INSTITUTE. Steffi was muttering about how Germans always found their way to good sites like these—Hittite ruins here—since the days when Ottomans used to let them do anything.

Steffi got out of the car first. "*Merhaba*," she said, in her bad Turkish, to the men digging. "*Guten tag.* Hello." They barely paused to look at her. Not ready for a chat.

Bruno stooped down to offer one of the men a cigarette, which he took. Bruno tried to tell him they just wanted to look—he acted this out with a hand at his brow—and the man pointed to the ridge of land behind him and said, "*Profesör.*"

They walked toward the ridge cautiously, trespassers relying on their Europeanness. Beyond them now they could see ancient colossal stone gateposts, with a growl-ing lion carved onto one and a more eroded animal (was it a lion too?) on the other portal. High walls of piled-up stones lined either side of a long path beyond the gates. Dieter had not expected to be thrilled to see this, but he was.

Sitting in a deck chair drinking from a thermos was a skinny fifty-year-old in khaki shorts and a T-shirt with a cartoon bunny on it—the professor. Bruno shook his hand. "We are amateurs of archaeology," Bruno told him, in German, "people of enthusiasm." Bruno always did the talking.

"I guess you know you're not supposed to be here," the man said, more or less amiably. "You can look from this spot. That's it."

The lions were guarding their city fiercely; anyone could see that. They had been doing this for something like 3,400 years. There were other gates beyond this; it had been a huge city, bigger than Athens. Dieter had once had to memorize Bible verses, and he knew that King David married Bathsheba, widow of Uriah the Hittite. That was about all he knew about Hittites, except that German scholars had deciphered their cuneiform writing, according to the books he used to read about alphabets.

On the way out, Bruno stopped to hand around his pack of cigarettes to all the workmen. He said, "Bruno," pointing to his chest, and shook their hands. Mehmet, Mustafa, Batur, some of them said. "Boğazkale," he told them, with his chin toward the town where the three of them were finally going to have lunch. "*Biz eski şeyler satın.*" We buy old things, and he was probably saying it wrong.

It wasn't much of a lunch at the café, toasted cheese sandwiches, but before they had finished their coffee, a man appeared at their table. He was a leathery old guy in a very worn sport jacket and a brown hat like a golf cap. "How are you?" he said in blurred English. "Maybe you want souvenirs."

"We collect old ones," Steffi said.

"You come to my store," he said. This turned out to be the place across the road with piles of shining new aluminum pots and pails and basins on display. Inside it was jam-packed (who bought all this?) and there was barely room for them to stand; only Steffi got a chair. He made tea nonetheless, which the men drank standing up. From under a wooden counter the shopkeeper brought out a package rolled in newspaper, which he unwrapped with so much care Dieter half-expected it to be alive. What was it? It was a flat slab of dried red clay the size of a playing card, with close rows of incised marks that looked like bird tracks. Holy shit. Cuneiform, Hittite writing. Look at the dug-in triangles and dashes, the straight horizontal lines of them.

"Fuck," Dieter said. "Oh, my God." Awe was bad for bargaining but this was way, way outside their usual.

And part of him was horrified—what was it *doing* in some guy's drawer?—this bit of terra-cotta so nakedly bearing the marks of a late–Bronze Age hand. Museums, of course, were filled with plunder. In London he'd seen the Rosetta Stone, that seven-hundred-kilo hunk of gray rock with three kinds of writing on it that Brits had triumphantly looted from Egypt. And in East Berlin, which he almost never crossed into, the Pergamon Museum had a whole Greek temple they'd hauled home to Germany from Turkey. Why was he shocked now?

"It's broken," Steffi said. The upper right corner had a piece chipped off, in a curve like the edge of a ski slope. "What do you want for it?"

And so it began. The man turned very angry at the first price Steffi named. He shouted something they couldn't understand. Steffi stayed calm. "We haven't come all this way to be yelled at," she said. "And how do we know the piece is real?" The man glowered and brought a magnifying glass from the drawer. Steffi gave it to Dieter, who made a show of examining the tablet, leaning close, taking off his eyeglasses to look. How porous and delicate the clay looked, how cleanly cut. He had no fucking idea. He gave a slow nod, as if he did.

The bargaining went back and forth. Bruno's eyes were excited, and he kept touching Steffi's arm. How much money did they have left? Probably not enough. At one point Steffi stood up—she was leaving, no deal. She was urged back, given more tea. In the end she offered an amount too close to all they had with them (seven hundred fifty deutschmarks) and when the man continued to scowl, she unhooked the gold locket from her neck and set it down before him. A stunning move, and it must've proven they really had no more cash, because the man gazed at all of them in turn and then said, "Okay, I see, yes."

All the way back through the rest of Turkey, across dicey, barely paved highways through the mountains and endless sandy roads along plains in the middle of nowhere, they were in danger of running out of money to buy gas and they ate only the cheapest kinds of food. They slept in the van, hidden behind trees; Bruno and Dieter took turns staying awake to keep guard. On one night, Steffi had to slip out of the van to pee, and she knocked over one of the amphorae, which had not been wrapped well enough and broke in several pieces.

Bruno called Steffi an ugly cunt too stupid to walk straight, after the amphora shattered. The fighting among them was worst in bare landscapes where there wasn't another living soul around to hear them. Steffi said Bruno was a sexual joke so in love with himself he didn't know the world was laughing at him. Dieter called them, more than once, the couple from hell. Bruno said Dieter was fooling no one with his high-minded smugness the whole time he was dying to stuff his pockets.

At Ipsala, the border crossing from Turkey into Greece, cars and trucks and buses were backed up for miles. Dieter had to keep turning the engine off so it didn't overheat. "I bet it's taking so long," Steffi said, "because they search so thoroughly."

"Please shut up," Bruno said.

"I can't stand this," Steffi said.

"Well, stand it," Dieter said. "You have to be cool when the guard is around. You have to."

"Steffi can do that," Bruno said. "She's used to being fake."

The guard they finally got was a stern-faced kid with a mustache who beckoned them out of the van. They had to show him the registration for the VW and all their passports, and then he poked his head inside the van and decided to make them unroll a carpet Steffi had bought.

"Isn't it beautiful?" Steffi said. The guard pointed to a suitcase and said something. He said it again, loudly—was he saying "Open," was it English?—and Dieter stepped forward to unzip the thing. *I shouldn't be here*, he was thinking. *I'm in a fucked-up situation I shouldn't be in, I'm ruining my life for the wrong thing.* How would Steffi ever manage in a Turkish jail? Bruno would get through it. Dieter didn't know about himself. The guard was saying something to them very sharply. What was it? Steffi's eyes were very still and scared; Bruno wasn't moving. Now the guard was waving his arm as if he were directing them back into their van. He said, *"Mach schnell,"* the one phrase in German people knew from movies. He wanted them to hurry, he wanted them out of the way. "Goodbye," he said. *"Auf wiedersehen."* Was it over? It was over. The engine coughed before it started up again. They rode like phantoms; none of them spoke.

Once they were on the Greek side, they were hooting and sighing and making jokes, happy culprits together. And in the first town in Greece, Steffi stole them a bottle of *retsina* to celebrate. They'd gone into a market to buy a loaf of bread and Steffi turned up back at the car, laughing as she pulled the wine bottle out from under her jacket. Bruno was furious—did she think they could take stupid chances? they couldn't take stupid chances!—but Dieter admired her nerve.

And Yugoslavia, which went on for a long time—it had

Macedonia, Serbia, Bosnia, Croatia, Slovenia—was full
of things to unnerve you, road signs depicting rockslides,
rumors of thieves, police, wolves. They cheered when they
crossed into Austria, and from there Bruno could send
to Germany for more cash while they waited in a border town. The waiting took longer than it should have,
and when Steffi wondered why, Bruno said he was sick of
her opinions and he was never going into business with a
woman again.

Steffi handled the insults with brisk counterattack—she
said, "Oh, fuck you," or "Don't be a prick every minute."
But Dieter felt sorry for her. Bruno was harsher all the
time, and the time wasn't up yet.

The van wasn't in great shape either, so when Bruno's
cash finally arrived, they had to have work done on its
poor engine before they drove the last stretch. At least
they could move into a cheap hotel for the night, take real
showers, eat a meal.

The joy of glasses of beer made them all act like the best
of friends at dinner. They toasted, they reminisced—
remember the old lady giving us soup in the farmhouse?
Remember when the border guy scared the shit out of all
of us? Steffi and Bruno finished each other's sentences. "A
trip we won't forget in a hurry," Bruno said.

In the middle of the night Dieter woke to a faint knocking at his door. Even half-asleep he knew it must be Steffi.
She stood in the hallway in her red kimono—on her face

was a crooked smile of assured naughtiness tinged with a little panic. Dieter, who'd answered the door in his underwear, beckoned her in. Quiet, quiet, they had to be quiet, Bruno was across the hall.

But it was sexy, all that stealth. Dieter felt at first that he was being kind to Steffi, he could be a lot kinder to her than Bruno, couldn't he, but he was excited as well. Under the robe she wore nothing, and the frankness of this seemed clever and wonderful. She had a lusher body than you would think in her clothes. Dieter hadn't been with a woman since leaving Berlin, and he hadn't entirely known how hungry he was.

They were trying to be soundless on the bed, and Steffi got the giggles and put her hand over her mouth, which made her laugh more. Dieter was past silliness by that time, too intent to be playful, and for a while they were on separate streams, friendly but estranged. He was thinking this really would have gone much better with Kiki; all his lusts in the past week had been for Kiki. He remembered the last night at the hotel in Ankara, lying in that bed and thinking of her, more than thinking. But now Steffi had come to him as a gift, and he remembered to have the sense to take it.

Of course, Bruno knew. How could he not know? When Dieter went down to breakfast the next day, Steffi was absent, and Bruno, looking up from his coffee, said, "It was her idea, wasn't it?"

Dieter shrugged. "I didn't stop her."

"I'm not asking what you didn't do," Bruno said. "It's time to leave her here. She can hitch home, she's so good at fending for herself."

Was this Bruno? He could be caustic in his hearty way but he'd never been cruel, in Dieter's long experience.

"You know she's been useful on this trip," Dieter said. "Her bargaining."

"We would've done fine without her. And now we will."

Leave Steffi behind, with no money at all, to get into strange cars across Austria and East Germany? Much about Steffi was annoying—her snap opinions, her talking too much, her faith in her own adorableness—but throwing her into danger was a whole other story. If they heard later that she'd met with real harm—raped, run over, taken up by Soviet pimps—how would either of them live with that forever? Bruno was never one to look ahead.

"Tell me you don't mean it," Dieter said.

Bruno gave him a very annoyed stare. "But I do."

"Okay, she's with me," Dieter said. "We're taking her. Because of me. Okay?"

Bruno laughed. "Your loss," he said.

The drive took a day and a night, and the two men took turns driving. Steffi was mostly silent. It was hard to tell how much threatening Bruno had done, but she was rattled and scared. *We're almost home*, each of them said several times, and Dieter was saying it to solace Steffi.

All her boldness seemed faded out of her. He watched the bend of her back, slumped against the door, in the T-shirt she'd been wearing for three days. At least they had the radio on—what a pleasure to hear German on the airwaves again. Bruno sang along to crappy East German stations; he'd done the vocals when he and Dieter had their band. Dieter tried not to sleep, even in the hours when he wasn't driving. He was watching over Steffi. Someone had to watch.

There was a very odd moment at the end of it all—the hot summer morning, Berlin bustling with everything that had been going on without them—when Bruno drew the van near the curb and stopped to drop Steffi off at her apartment at the edge of Kreuzberg. Who was going to help her with her luggage? Was anyone kissing her goodbye? Not Bruno, who said, "See you," and looked straight ahead. Dieter carried the rolled rug Steffi had bought and one of the duffels up the stairs of her building. He was startled when she flung herself at him in passionate farewell. What a romantic adventure she thought they'd had. Her body did have a sweet abundance, even in the sweaty shirt, and he patted her back with what he hoped felt like affection.

And it wasn't even farewell—they were business partners, the three of them. That at least was a matter of honor. And each piece they'd brought back seemed to require its own negotiations. They went as a trio to dealers, collectors,

middlemen. They told people they had bought these remarkable whatevers from a once-rich Turkish family in
London and sometimes they said Geneva. No one wanted
to know too much. Steffi had bouts of being perky, trying
to charm gallery owners with tales of British pubs, but
Bruno and Dieter kept her back when they could. She ir-
ritated both of them. Bruno would say, "That's enough,
Steffi."

Outside the selling, Dieter still stopped by her apartment from time to time to check on her. He lived way over
on the other side of Berlin, near Charlottenburg, and he
thought it was very good of him to come so far. Her place
was a mess; she herself was sort of a mess now. The friend
whose chic little clothing store she'd worked in wasn't hir-
ing her back and she was still adjusting to losing Bruno.
"Don't you think he's a turd? Don't answer. He's a turd."
Dieter would listen to her—she was manic between bouts
of listlessness—until he had to say, "Okay, take a bath,
I'm cleaning the kitchen, we're going out." In this way he
grew attached to her.

One wouldn't think any of this had much power in it.
How could a mercy-fuck be anyone's longed-for darling?
Yet he and Steffi often slept together, at the end of those
nights, and this fooling around had sparks. The old Steffi
arose then, ready for anything. And grateful to Dieter.
They'd fall asleep fondly entwined, and the fondness was
real.

Some cash was starting to come in from the Turkish
purchases. They'd guessed wrong about many things—the

amphora wasn't as much of a prize as they'd thought, but some of the Byzantine coins brought surprisingly high amounts. The big disappointment was the Hittite tablet. In a cool-white showroom off Kurfürstendamm, with nooks lit like shrines, an elderly woman dealer wound in a paisley scarf said, "So wonderful!" and offered them no more than what they'd paid. They went to two other dealers and Steffi finally got someone up to a thousand deutschmarks. In New York, where Steffi kept saying she wanted to go, that would be less than seven hundred dollars, she pointed out. Not so much, split three ways.

But that was the last of their antiquities, and, really, they had done very well. Bruno had them celebrating with a few bottles of very decent Riesling at a restaurant he liked. He was already seeing someone named Marie, that Steffi wasn't supposed to know about yet. For some reason, Bruno had never said Dieter was a bad friend for sleeping with Steffi. It was true that Steffi was not the first girl they'd both had sex with, but the other had been when they were much younger and not serious. Were they serious now? Maybe Steffi was. In the restaurant, while Dieter toasted to adventures in crime, she gazed into his eyes over her glass. She was wearing a darker lipstick than usual and earrings like key chains. She looked pretty—she *was* pretty, in an ordinary way. And she had more to spend on herself now.

They all looked better. In this stage, the smuggling was making them very pleased with themselves. Dieter thought that in those self-help books people bought in America, the ones about how to gain total confidence and never worry, the secret advice should be to go break laws. Look at Bruno, handsome and groomed, a blond hero merrily chewing his expensive veal. Look at himself, Dieter, always the quiet, wary one, at ease in the restaurant's imperial banquette, airing his views on the nature of the soul, a topic he never would've raised before. And even Steffi, recently so unraveled and depressed, was a calmer, more queenly version of her sometimes loud self.

Dieter was saying that the word *soul* was a fuzzy term, a bit of bad poetry that stood for an actual inward consciousness. This made Steffi laugh. "Are you in high school?" she said. "Who cares?"

Bruno was also chuckling, which was the nicest he'd been to Steffi in a while. "Dieter," he said, "is very soulful."

Steffi seemed to think this was hilarious. "Look at Dieter," she said. The celebration was going to their heads.

I'm surrounded by assholes, Dieter thought. Their faces were bizarre to him then, the stretched mouths and narrow eyes. And the others could tell. They were coarse but they weren't stupid.

"You won't do a trip like this again," Bruno said. "But I might."

"No, you won't," Steffi said. "You don't know enough."

"Dieter dreams of repaying the noble Turks," Bruno said, "but he likes the money just fine."

Dieter hadn't especially thought about paying anyone back—who would he send money to? The pots-and-pans salesman from Boğazkale? The government? But he was aware that he was holding on to his money, thus far, as if he might have to do that.

The others ran through their profits with all due speed. Bruno dispensed his to the dealers of much more expensive drugs than he'd used before and went to bars day and night like a job. Steffi never made it to New York, but she got herself to Paris, where the alleged glories of the city disappointed her but she came back with clothes she was very crazy about. Dieter didn't have a fashion eye, but he could see she looked "smart" in them (as English people said), assured and alert and sleek. She was still interested in Dieter. She sent him postcards from Paris—"sunsets on the Seine not as good as in Turkey"—and when she was back in Berlin, Dieter began again to pay visits to her apartment, long talks followed by getting into bed. The bed part was better than ever, actually.

"Are you in love with her?" his friend Ulrich asked.

Dieter was stunned by the question. What kind of romantic comedy did his friend think he was in? Dieter couldn't imagine *falling* for a person like Steffi, though he hoped someone would someday; he wished her well. "We have a particular friendship, with an erotic element," he said. "We don't even like each other that much. It's definitely not love."

Ulrich thought if they were having good sex without really liking each other, it was probably love.

"Hah," Dieter said.

They were doing fine until it went on too long. As the rainy spring weather turned warmer, Steffi announced that it was almost the anniversary of their getting together. "June a year ago you were with Bruno," Dieter said. "You're not thinking of celebrating with him?"

Steffi did not take this well, and he was sorry he'd said it. He had to apologize; he had to say he was glad they'd started whatever they had, which was almost true.

"Don't do me any favors," Steffi said.

But she believed the pileup of their months together meant something, whether he was willing to admit it or not. Being Steffi, she thought she knew what he didn't.

"*Mein Schatz*," she said. My treasure.

That definitely was not what he wanted to be called. She was going to ruin what they had with falsity.

And she was always broke now. She was back in another dress store, earning too little for someone like her. Dieter had finally used his hoard of cash to buy a new light table and to rent a bigger studio with another graphic designer, and by this time he was starting to get more work, good work. The long hours at it made him impatient with Steffi. Or something did. Couldn't she not talk only about stupid TV shows; couldn't she refrain from putting her muddy shoes on his rug; couldn't she stop smoking cigarettes in bed? She could, but not happily.

And yet she wanted more of this unhappiness. She wanted to see him more often, she wanted to meet all his friends. Ulrich said, "Well, she's lively." Ulrich lived with a woman who had a three-year-old boy and Steffi played tag with the boy all over the living room. It was nice of her, and she did look pretty in the heat of the chase.

"He's going to marry her, I bet," Steffi said, when they were back in Dieter's apartment that night. "People do that, you know."

"Never heard of it." Dieter had taken some care not to lead her on.

She looked hurt (as well she might) but then her expression changed to something wily and defiant, and she reached for him in a long, undulant, full-body hug. Dieter understood that his arousal was going to be used to prove her point, but he was aroused nonetheless. That was just the way it was. It wasn't until afterward that the thought came to him that she was really quite capable of getting pregnant on purpose.

And a week later he was out with Bruno, who was already looking like hell and never had anything good to say about Steffi, when they decided they had to go eat in a Turkish restaurant. Bruno had found one in Neukölin, in the American sector, a dark, rustic little place with posters of the Bosporus at sunset. They were the only Germans there, and they were lustily chomping on delicious kebabs, when two very pretty blonde women walked in. There was a noisy table of teenagers on the other side of them, but Bruno could overhear the women debating the menu. "Adana is the name of a city," he leaned across to tell them. "The kebab mix is a little spicier there." He said Adana correctly, with the accent on the first syllable.

Bruno said, "It's an interesting city." He was perking up for the girls.

And what terrific girls they turned out to be. They were both schoolteachers—they had Turkish kids in their classes—and they were certainly a big improvement, in beauty and hipness, over anyone who ever taught Dieter. Gisela, the skinnier one, taught art and asked extremely good questions about what Dieter did, and the tall one, Birgit, was a skier and clearly liked Dieter too. Such a thing hadn't happened to him in a long time (two girls) and had to do with how bad Bruno looked now. Dieter heard himself getting ebullient and talking on and on; he held forth about the Muslim view of the soul, you could see it in the way mosques were constructed. "They know about geometry," Gisela said. And so he chose Gisela, which was one of the most intelligent things he ever did.

Steffi did not take it well. For a while he saw both women, to avoid being too rash, but soon enough he couldn't get through another night with Steffi. Steffi was furious when she heard the news. Her face was clenched into what looked like real hate. "You shit. You know what a shit you are?" she said. "You just take what you can get and leave."

"What did I take?" he said.

The question made her yowl. "I have no value at all to you. You have to say that too?"

"Steffi," he said, more or less gently. He couldn't remember why he'd ever bothered to be with her, but he wanted to be his better self here, as if Gisela were watching. He kept feeling, actually, that Gisela was watching.

"I should call your new girlfriend and warn her about you," Steffi said.

What did she want from him? Did she think he could unsay what he'd said? He was truly in love, for the first time in his life, but if Gisela ever wanted him to leave, he thought that he would simply go. All this greed and fury, all this grasping, where would it ever get Steffi? She was repeating and insisting. The futile noise of it made Dieter cold at heart.

She never phoned Gisela (not that she even knew Gisela's name but she could've found out) and she only phoned Dieter once, to demand that he give back a hairbrush she'd left at his apartment. Dieter found it behind the sink and brought it across town to her. Steffi stood in the doorway with her hand out for the brush. "About time," she said. When he told her to take care of herself, she said, "What's it to you?"

He thought afterward about how hardened and stringy she looked. He began to think he should give her something to prove to her that he'd valued her, although he'd never valued her. Not money, of course, but maybe a savings bond. No, that was too weird and familial. Maybe jewelry? That would mislead her. Maybe something that had to do with Turkey? He began looking into the stores in Turkish neighborhoods. There were silk scarves, but not ones Steffi would wear; there were brass coffee beakers and tea sets with gold-trimmed glass cups. She had loved the apple tea the carpet sellers poured for customers, and he saw boxes of it, loose leaves, tea bags, instant granules, labeled with pictures of bright red and green apples. He walked out of a shop with fourteen boxes of different kinds, all they had, and sent them at once by mail to Steffi. *Enjoy this. Dieter.*

She never answered. Had she moved? He heard not. Was she insulted? It wasn't much of a present maybe, but certainly not meant as an insult. Did he want thanks, was that creepy of him? He felt ridiculous and also cheap, and he certainly never told Gisela.

He didn't talk much to Gisela about women he'd been with before. It was all beginning so well between them, there was no need to tell all his stories. But sometimes Gisela asked why he'd stayed with Steffi so long. It wasn't so long, he said, it wasn't so bad, whatever they didn't have hadn't seemed so important. Gisela looked confused. (If love wasn't important, what was?) She never pressed him—she had a lovely, calm temperament. For the rest of his life he considered her his greatest stroke of luck. And he secretly believed that if she'd never walked into that restaurant, he might've stayed with Steffi forever. And not with good results. He'd fallen into a truthful life, but it might have been otherwise. Sincerity hadn't come as naturally to him as it did to some people. Dear Gisela had no idea.

Gisela pretty much trusted him from the first, and she wasn't an especially naive person; her own history included some dark and callous types. Once, when they were out drinking with some friends of hers from school, Dieter made a reference to once having been a great smuggler, and he saw they all thought he was joking. Even when he said, "But really," they laughed. Gisela had always known to believe him—the ways of the world generally didn't shock her—but she used to say, "You know you would've been caught if you'd kept it up."

"Who would've caught me, who'd bother?" he said.

"Someone," she said.

And sometimes Dieter had dreams about this—a prison that was a tunnel with walls of slime, a path he couldn't turn around in, and a woman calling out to him from another room.

Dieter was in his fifties when he traveled to America for the first time. A client had hired him to design the logo and signage for a new hotel not yet built, and there was some feeling that he had to see its setting. What a jumble New York was, on first sight. Did no one pick up those piles of garbage? He was told the city had improved greatly. But wasn't Midtown an expensive neighborhood? He was there in July, and the streets smelled of rot in the heat.

He wondered if Kiki the American had stayed in Turkey all this time or if she'd come back to New York by now. She wasn't still on the farm; he didn't think so. If he ever met her, he would show her the pictures of his children. Max was studying history; Silke wanted to be a dancer. In their pictures they looked very alive, with bright eyes and rumpled scarves and open faces. Gisela looked wonderful too—older, more angular, and now with wine-red hair, a change she'd begun as defiance. When the chemo made her hair fall out and it grew back in chunks, she went auburn. Her hair was longer now, an aureole of jagged fuzz, still punk maroon.

She'd been in New York when she was young, and she told him, "Anything goes there. If you walk out naked it won't get any attention."

"You did that?"

"Not quite," she said.

Bruno had told him New Yorkers gave spectacular parties. Bruno looked more ravaged than ever, though he was probably going to live longer than Gisela. Bruno had gotten a second wind after the Berlin Wall fell; there were bars now that didn't know him, an influx of foreigners with nothing against him. "Even the dirt is sexy in New York," he said to Dieter.

•

Dieter was not in what anyone would call a party mood.
He had been very reluctant to leave Gisela, despite her
claims that she felt fine and needed no tending. He missed
her during every meal he ate alone and he was phoning
her too often. And he hated the hours with the clients,
who were too American, too childish in their showing
off. The summer heat beat down meanly on him whenever he walked outside. On his free day he had the sense
to retreat to a museum, waiting for the art, any art, to
help him with ideas. American air-conditioning was really very good.

His best moment was when he walked up the majestic
stairway to the second floor of the Met; he loved the glorious spaces of old exhibition halls. Not that they knew
about old here, with buildings always being blasted and
rebuilt higher. How did people in this city keep track of
themselves, with so much coming at them at once? No
wonder Kiki had told him she liked the quiet in Turkey.
He thought the lettering he designed for the hotel should
actually look dense and busy and excited.

The galleries of Ancient Near Eastern Art very con-
veniently had a case displaying writing and alphabets.
Silver ingots with raised hieroglyphics on them, quartzite
cylindrical seals to roll out letters. There was even a cuneiform tablet, circa fourteenth to thirteenth century BC,
very much like the one they'd bargained for so ineptly in
Turkey. It had the top three rows of writing with a line
under them, as theirs had, and it even had a chipped corner curved like a ski slope. Maybe it *was* their piece. It

was the record of a lawsuit—someone had been able to read it. HITTITE MIDDLE KINGDOM, PROVENANCE CENTRAL ANATOLIA, PURCHASED 1985. Could it be theirs? The more he looked, the more he thought so.

Museums weren't always so careful who they bought from. He'd missed out on getting whatever sum it was sold for—but he did feel proud to see it. He wanted to tell Steffi, who'd done the bargaining, who'd given her gold locket for it. (Not that he knew where Steffi was.) *Hey, it was a good piece after all,* he'd say to her. Would she care? What was important? Look at all this labeled debris. All things faded and crumbled and came to dust—he was in a museum of immaculate dust—and nothing was exactly gone. This wasn't even comforting but it seemed apparent to him.

The tablet was becoming more familiar by the second and also more handsome as an object. He was feeling very fond of all these shards and beads and bowls on display, these fragments and remnants. What touching little pieces of human effort they were, all of them, the tablet with its careful grooves listing some petulant lawsuit. How fragile.

He was sorry he couldn't touch it, couldn't unlock the vitrine and feel the marks in the clay. He remembered Kiki, when they first showed her one of the amphorae—how afraid she was to let her hand even graze it, how reverent she was about its age. If she lived in New York, as she very well might, she probably came here—these galleries would draw her, after all those years in Turkey. Maybe she'd gazed at the tablet many times and admired it—it was a thing she'd admire, it was quite amazing—without knowing at all he ever had anything to do with it. How could she know? The thought made him feel quite happily modest.

7

Monika was amazed at what Hurricane Sandy did to New York. The sheer sound of the wind was like nothing she'd heard before. Her friends from Europe sent her worried emails (they thought New York was a disaster zone anyway). Monika made fun of their messages. "They thought I was swimming in the subway," she told Lynnette. "I did almost have to move a tree that fell in front of my building. It took them a week to come get it."

"City would've heard from me if it took that long," Lynnette said. "And I would've gotten the TV news on them too."

For the past few years Monika had been going to Lynnette to get her eyebrows shaped. The waxing and plucking took longer than it should have, but she'd become a big fan of Lynnette's personality. Lynnette had stories—about boyfriends, bosses, random passersby—and the moral of all of these stories was that nobody fucked with her. "Got to set people straight," she said. Monika, who was not like this herself, always left the salon with the bracing feeling that she was in fact exactly like this.

Today Lynnette was going on about certain people who wanted credit for doing nothing special. "They think they're saints. And everybody else is trash." This referred, it turned out, to the woman who'd been seeing Lynnette's ex and now was visiting him weekly in a "facility." "Like she should get a medal for that."

Monika knew the facility was jail. Three weeks ago, Lynnette had mouthed the word "Rikers" when she'd had to explain a story she'd gone too far in. People tended to tell Monika things. She was in her early thirties now, and she looked (even with superb eyebrows) very reliable, which she was.

She had her eyes closed, while Lynnette, with professional deftness, stroked on the wax. One of the other patrons had said that Lynnette was an artist, a bit of hyperbole Monika never echoed because she was, in her working life, an art historian. She worked part-time at the Met now and had almost managed to explain to Lynnette just what she did: provenance research, which meant figuring out which objects in the museum's collection had been stolen. She was extra qualified because her first language was German, and the art she was charged with investigating had been moved around during the Nazi era. She was supposed to find and read records of seized property, pore over dealers' sales, see the patterns of smugglers.

"Are you like a cop?" Lynnette said.

"We don't put people in jail. The criminals are mostly dead."

"Why do you do it then?"

"For justice," Monika said. "And it looks bad for a museum to keep stolen goods."

"Doesn't look that bad to me," Lynnette said.

As a student Monika had certainly thought that most European museums were full of ancient art looted by colonial powers from countries down on their luck in later centuries. Didn't look bad to most people. But the objects she was researching now had been confiscated from Jewish collectors, Jewish families, Jewish art dealers; they had been offered in desperation, abandoned in flight, or stripped from homes of the transported; they had blood on them.

"If someone stole that nice leather jacket of yours," Monika said, "wouldn't you want it sent back?"

"I pity the fool," Lynnette said, "tries to steal my jacket."

Monika repeated this to her husband that night. He loved dialogue like that, and he had been acting a little bored by her conversation lately. She didn't imitate Lynnette too closely—Monika had been in New York since college and was noticeably German only on words with *th* in them, but she would've sounded like a racist comic if she'd tried for Lynnette's rhythms.

Her husband could imitate anyone. He was a visual artist, not an actor, but he had a goofy satiric accuracy. When
they were first together, his style of joking put her into
fits of helpless laughter. She hadn't been raised in a stuffy
way but still America had seemed much more lighthearted
than the Berlin of her youth. She wrote to her mother,
"Everyone is younger here."

Now Julian, her husband, said, "Someone should steal
her jacket to teach her a lesson."

"What a mean thing to say. Why do you say that?"

"I just get tired of people thinking they're above every
kind of trouble. You can get like that, you know, with
your job."

He'd been doing this lately, getting hostile from nowhere. His gallery had dropped him seven months ago,
which was naturally upsetting, but he'd had plenty of ups
and downs before. And none of it was Monika's fault. *Au
contraire*, she was his helpmate; he had a teaching job at
adjunct's pay, and her salary was carrying them.

It occurred to her that he was probably not having an
affair if he was being so openly irritable. She thought that
men who were being sneaky were more likely to be blandly
agreeable at home, even cheerful. But, then, he acted like
someone looking for evidence against her, so he might be
getting ready, tallying excuses.

These were just theories, but something not good was
happening. In earlier days they had split up and gotten
back together a few times, so she did know him. Some of

the breakups had been fast and brief but the last one had come very close to severing them for good. He was still outraged at her for certain things.

Lately that outrage was mixed in with his rancor and grief at losing the gallery. Sometimes she thought very highly of him—his talent, his work habits, his stubbornness about not yielding to art-world trends—but now was not a time when she admired him.

And her job hadn't turned her into a spoiled princess—what was he talking about? She'd grown up scrappy-poor with a nutty single mother; she took nothing for granted. Or almost nothing. He knew that.

"Don't be mean," she said to him. Lynnette would've come out with something snappier.

But he surprised her. "I don't want to be," he said. "I don't." He said it so nicely too.

The next time she saw Lynnette, three weeks later, things were much better with Julian. She heard herself bragging. "You know what he did? He built a desk for me in the corner of our bedroom. A built-in desk." He was actually a decent carpenter but it was rare for him to bother with a practical project.

"I had a boyfriend used to build things," Lynnette said. She meant the one before the last one—she liked to mention him. "Isaiah built me a shelf. I still have it in the kitchen; it's very solid."

Monika thought any idiot could build a shelf but she certainly wasn't saying that. Even Lynnette had a heart, and Isaiah seemed to be the one who had broken it.

"And for Claude's birthday one year he made a special cake stand, tall as me."

Claude, her brother, was the only other person Lynnette spoke of with unbarbed love. He had told Lynnette that once he was making money (which he wasn't yet), he'd set her up in her own brow bar. "I won't need billions or anything," Lynnette said. "Just the security deposit and a few month's rent. It could happen."

"I'll follow you," Monika said. "Of course."

The salon where Lynnette now labored over people like Monika was a big place in the East Fifties where you could get hair removed from any part of you, in very private rooms, or makeup artfully applied for special occasions. It smelled of perfume and chemicals and melted wax and had clinical white tables and glass bowls with petals floating in them. What would Lynnette's be like?

"Better music," Lynnette said. Here they played soft rock very softly. "And I'd make it green, like a shade of chartreuse but not bright. The color green is relaxing."

Monika had different ideas about color but she was impressed that Lynnette had thought this through; you'd never guess she was someone with a dream. At her age, what had Monika wanted? Only Julian. Sex, sex, sex, love, love, love. She'd lingered in the U.S. because of him. Everyone thought the reunified Berlin was so hip, and parts of it were—what was left of the ruins in the East with their squatters and clubs and graffiti. But would Julian ever have moved there? Not a chance. Berlin sort of gave him the creeps. He believed in New York.

"He has strong ideas," her mother said, when she met him on her first visit. "So make him think you're listening but don't listen."

Her mother was often full of cagey advice, though her own sorry love life wasn't much of a credential. Monika thought of her as someone who was ineffectively bossy, laying down the law to a series of men who simply shrugged off her demands. Most of them had been fairly nice to Monika when she was little, and even her father (no one was sure if he was her father) brought her presents when he showed up every few years. Bruno (she certainly never called him *Papa* or *Vati*) was an old boyfriend who'd reunited with her mother for a very brief fling, some thirty-one years ago. Alcohol had aged him ever since, gouging out his face and making slits of his eyes, but he wasn't a bad guy. "Steffi, Steffi," he liked to say to her mother, "at least we're still alive." A little maudlin, but he could carry it.

The other thing her mother had said about Julian right away was, "He likes himself."

"That can be a good thing," Monika said. "Not like us. Not like Germans."

Whole libraries had been written on the ways Germans carried the shame of their history. It could be complicated to find out which grandparents had done what in the Nazi years, but didn't every family have a perpetrator in it somewhere? A cousin. A lost enthusiast. An alternate self.

Americans felt surprisingly free to quiz Monika about exactly that, and indeed there was a great-uncle she'd heard the worst about. Julian had asked right away (he had his reasons), but then he didn't like hearing it always brought up by other people. He'd go silent then. As if the past was best left unsaid.

Not that he was quiet by nature. He'd been trained, in his schooling, to fearlessly defend his art (installations that needed huge amounts of space) and had done well with women too by not bothering to hesitate. In the beginning she'd liked all that blurting confidence.

In his current season of blighted hope he didn't talk so much. His tendency to forge ahead, to commandeer, took the form of doing things to their apartment, a nest of rambling rooms in Brooklyn (on a mixed block in Bushwick), which was much enhanced by his improvised solutions, his handy-dandy storage and stacks of wooden boxes. He was also doing a lot of sketching, getting some new ideas that seemed to please him vastly; she wasn't a huge fan of his art, actually, though she said she was. And maybe she would get to be someday. He was the great love of her life, for all his crap. She did think that.

In the winter of a year and a half ago she had left him. He had brought it on himself (in her view) by weeks of disdain and sullen fights about money, and she had run off with a gallery owner who was too old and not remotely serious about her. He'd taken her to Saint Barts for a week; she'd never been to the Caribbean and the tropics in winter had truly dazzled her, but by the end she only wanted Julian. She had to work very hard to get him back—remorse, anguish, promises, all of it authentic—and this had taken till the spring. A terrible time. But once the pact was made, the reunion was joyous on both sides and sexy.

The gallery owner, whose name was Richard, had not taken this well. She had left too soon for his liking, and whenever they ran into each other he was barely civil to her and transparently rude to Julian. During that Caribbean week, she had voiced certain opinions to him about Julian that she now regretted. Julian, in his way, was forever convinced that grants had failed to go to him, invitations to group shows, sales to collectors, because Richard had put some sort of kibosh on him. And he might have been just a little bit right.

She would have done anything to remove Richard as an obstacle. She would have connived or bribed or slept with him again but she didn't think that was how it worked at this point.

She asked Lynnette, "When you've done something stupid, do you try to make up for it eventually? Like if you mess something up?"

Lynnette said, "If you think I ever mess up people's eyebrows, I do not. You wouldn't suggest that, right?"

"No! Of course not. I'm thinking more about a friend I offended."

"My brother went and bought me a new pair of sun-
glasses when he stepped on mine. That was good, wasn't it?"

"Extremely."

"He was afraid I'd kill him," Lynnette said.

Julian, who was clearly trying to draw himself out of
depression by being industrious around the house, had
begun building an elaborate cupboard, and Monika re-
spected this. He was suffering the indignities of rejection
and he was trying not to just suffer. They had good eve-
nings together now; they sat on the couch drinking beer
and he explained at length the new installation he was
designing, for a school if a school ever asked him, something with birches and barbed wire that didn't sound
so bad.

At seven in the morning, while she was stepping out
of the shower and Julian was still asleep, her phone rang.
What kind of jerk called at that hour? A man's voice,
speaking German—it was Bruno, of all people. He was
fine, thank you, but her mother was not so good. She was
in the hospital, a heart attack. "It wouldn't be such a bad
idea to come home," he said. Monika wanted to speak to
her—why was she talking to Bruno, that pickled blur of a
person, and not her mother? Her mother was sleeping, he
said, and still a bit weak for talking. "I think come now
and not later," he said.

•

"She's not that *old*," Monika wailed to Julian.

Julian was hugging her, patting her back. "We'll go right away," he said.

He'd only been to Germany with her once, and he'd hated it, all the conversations that had to stop and change to English, all the art he thought was too cerebral or too stylized or too something. He had never really wanted to go. And her mother had given him a hard time. Her mother wouldn't want him there.

"You have your classes to teach," Monika said.

"Who gives a fuck?" he said.

She would send for him if it looked really bad, she said, but she didn't think it was so bad. He was insulted—his face went cold—but he said, "Okay, it's your call." And he got up to make coffee for her, while she tried to phone airlines to get a special rate for family illness. She sounded businesslike in a crazy way and then her voice broke when she had to give her mother's name.

For more than seven hours on the plane she thought about her mother. When she was little, Monika went with her mother every day to the dress store she managed and played quietly in the back. Her mother was very sharp with her if no one was there and was always perkier with people around. Once, when she was nine, her mother disappeared for two days and left her alone. Monika had known to knock on a neighbors' door; they were a big family with older kids, she was fine. Nobody wanted a mother who unraveled like that, and in her teens Monika had run away twice with boys but never for long. Her best wasn't good enough but her mother had done her best. On the phone, she still called Monika *Mausi*, little mouse. And she'd always had her moments of festive silliness—they danced in circles in the kitchen after a certain man called. The memory of that made Monika tearful on the plane.

Monika could tell that she was overpreparing for bad news, planning how to carry herself when she reached the hospital. In fact, when she walked into the room, her mother was awake, with her head propped up on the pillows, trying to explain something to a woman who turned out to be her friend, Elke.

"My God!" her mother squeaked, when she recognized Monika. "I must be dying, for you to come all this way." She went into a toothy smile; she was reaching to hug her.

"You don't look as bad as I thought you would," Monika said.

"Your mother is getting much better," Elke said.

It was a grand relief. Monika felt heady from the joy of it, the luck.

"Are they giving you drugs?" she asked. "Something good, I hope. Can they keep this from happening again?"

"I have to stop smoking," her mother said. "I've stopped before. Done it a hundred times."

"She has to take it easy," Elke said. "Which is not her disposition."

Her mother looked frowsy and defeated; she had been dyeing her hair a scratchy shade of ash blonde, which was growing out. She was round-shouldered and fleshy and somehow still thin.

"How long are you staying?" she said.

Bruno was nowhere in sight. He'd absented himself once he summoned the others. Elke stayed till after lunch, and another old friend, Christa, came after suppertime. In between conversations, her mother slept.

Monika sat by the bed, hearing the TV news the room's other patient had turned on, and watching her mother's sleeping face, sealed in its own realm. She'd spoken to the doctor, a woman no older than she was, who was very cheerful about how her mother had responded to treatment. She was out of the woods, as Americans liked to say. The doctor did not use that metaphor but Monika thought of those woods—the dark forest, the thicket of danger always in wait.

On the phone, she had to explain to Julian that German hospitals didn't throw people out after a few days like American ones, and she had to stay to get her mother settled at home. "All my mother talks about is Bruno, as if he personally saved her by showing up eventually."

"Give your mom my love," he said.

Her mother had never been friendly to him. She had not forgiven Monika for moving to the U.S. and was always telling her how much cheaper and more socially advanced

Berlin was, and the men had better manners. She was anti-American in politics, too, partly out of her grudge against the marriage.

"And don't run off with any German guys," Julian said. He'd heard the stories about her mother.

Monika had grown up in Kreuzberg, a part of Berlin that should've been East on the map but was in the Western sector, shabby and Bohemian and also popular with Turkish families. When she was little, there were flea markets selling old clothes, squatters in wrecked buildings, and the streets smelled of smoke from the coal stoves everyone used for heat. The neighborhood had changed, but not entirely. Food sales had grown more lavish, but she saw plenty of familiar stores. She was peering over the gate of a school she'd once gone to when she almost tripped on a square of brass set in the pavement. It was a "stumble stone," engraved with local history. *Here lived Viktoria Kanafa year of birth 1895 murdered 1940 place unknown.*

She was going to take a picture of it with her phone, to send to Julian, but she'd sent him too many such photos already. His dislike of Berlin had everything to do with his being Jewish, and who could argue with that? But she wanted him to see the way the city made an effort, in this century. A giant menorah in front of the Brandenburg Gate every Hanukkah, a Holocaust Memorial as big as three football fields. She had wondered (or friends had) if her mother's lobbying against Julian had an anti-Semitic taint, but there was no sign of that. Her mother was a left-ist, noisy and open-minded and cosmopolitan, a marcher for civil rights, nothing close to skinhead about her.

The apartment was rumpled but not dirty. And too familiar—the blond wood coffee table with a cigarette burn at one edge, the blue-and-brown Turkish rug. In the bedroom, there was a bra thrown over a chair, a paper-back on the floor, the unmade bed from which her mother had phoned for her own ambulance. Monika wasn't in the habit of feeling sorry for her mother—they'd had a life together of accusing, blocking, opposing—but a wash of sorrow came over her now. Her mother had called Bruno during the wait for the ambulance, left a message he picked up hours later. Not someone she saw that much, but he was a man.

And he'd been all right, for him. Two days after Monika's arrival he showed up again at the hospital, and her mother crowed from her bed—"Look who's here!" It was years since Monika had seen him, but he was so battered and sunken and leathery he wasn't really aging anymore.

"Both my girls!" he said, as he hugged each of them.

Monika used to wonder if she looked like him. Maybe the small nose? Impossible to tell now.

"You know Monika is a big success now," her mother said. "She works at the Metropolitan Museum of Art."

"It's just a temporary job," Monika said. "I think it's ending soon."

She tried to explain provenance research and did better in German. Bruno seemed perfectly familiar with it.

"Very good work," he said. "They can never give back, but they have to try. And your husband is fine?"

Her mother sighed.

"Julian's getting quite a name for himself," Monika said. "He does these big installations, you know, site-specific work that uses natural and man-made elements in really startling ways, and he's shown in a number of really very good places." There were a few bits of truth embedded in this.

"You have to bring him here," Bruno said. "I know people who would be interested, gallery people. Berlin likes that kind of thing."

Had she learned bullshitting from Bruno? It was always tempting to believe him, and never a good idea. Since when was he a beloved crony of big movers in the art world? He did know people, from being a fixture in various drinking venues all those years, but those weren't real bonds and they'd run out by now anyway.

"I'll send photos of what he does," she said, "to your phone."

"You're doing a business deal in my sickroom?" her mother gasped at them. "This is how you visit me? You're in a cardiology unit!"

"Steffi, Steffi," Bruno said. "Can I get you something nice to eat? Maybe one of those puddings from a Turkish restaurant? You like them, they're not too heavy."

"I raised a little capitalist," her mother said. "She

always wanted to be not so poor. Look at how she dresses now. Like she owns the world. Grab and take, that's her."

"Can you not do this?" Monika said. Why couldn't she have a mother who didn't escalate every dialogue?

"You know what's a really good kind of pudding?" Bruno said. "There's an almond one that's really good."

"They won't have that in this neighborhood," her mother said.

"They might. Monika can go out and check. Yes?"

Did Bruno think her mother was waiting for time alone with him? They weren't a couple, but she might like his sole attention, being who she was. Even now she might.

Monika was just as glad to be out-of-doors, wandering the upscale byways of Mitte in search of something Turkish. And her mother was asleep by the time she got back. Bruno was gone—no need to stay with a snoring patient—but he had texted her. *Meet for a drink tonight?* She was having dinner with a girlfriend, but late night was not too late for Bruno.

He looked like the ghost of glory days past, in that bustling bar, with his wintry-white head easily visible. He whistled at her outfit—people still whistled?—and he ordered the kind of beer he remembered she liked three years ago.

"I hope you don't mind, but I have to ask. What did the doctors say?"

"They seemed optimistic," she said. "If she changes her habits, if she takes the drugs."

Bruno shook his head. "She won't let you see, but she was crying from being scared. She says it's not good. Not at all."

"She does?"

Was her mother making this up, in her way, or had Monika not gotten it right? In her head, she was going over the language the doctor had used. Myocardial infarction, ischemia, scarring.

"I'll talk to them again," she said.

"You have money?" he said. "She doesn't have any money."

The government would send nurses to visit, and she would get some small pension if she couldn't work. That wasn't enough?

"Not anymore," Bruno said.

"I'm not very rich," Monika said. She was wearing a clever black dress she had bought for work, on sale at Barneys. It threw everybody off.

"It would mean a lot to her," Bruno said. "Whatever you can. Online it's very easy to send money now."

Was she being scammed? She thought suddenly of Lynnette, always on the alert for scams. Had her mother put Bruno up to this? Or was this Bruno's idea?

"If you don't have it, it's okay," he said. "I just want her to be comforted. Money comforts people."

Monika laughed.

"So you'll go back soon," he said. "To New York. You live there now. I understand this. We can't be two places at once, only gods can."

Monika was smiling, because he said it as if he might once have made this mistake.

"Now," he said, "so you know about the art fair in the fall here. It's late to get a gallery to sponsor your husband, but I think it could happen."

"He would be so happy."

"Yes," Bruno said. "Success makes people happy. But some of us live without it." He had a tone between rue and enlightenment.

"You get by."

"Oh," he said, "I have my ways."

Horror came over her that night, as she lay in the dark, on a couch in the living room of the mother that she had complained about all her life. She'd been too hopeful, too sure doctors could fix things, too American. Her mother had hardly ever been someone she depended on, but none of that was the point. The point was very serious.

How stupid she had been not to let Julian come with her. She missed him very much. Only a stupid person would do this alone.

But did Bruno really know what was going on? Or was he scaring her for profit, a truly hideous idea? No, that was too much even for him. If there was a conniving spirit, it was her mother. And you couldn't blame her for wailing to Bruno, for crying in fear, for insisting the worst was coming soon. People did that. Having a mother like that made you used to what people did.

•

And Monika could not get a straight answer out of the doctor at the hospital. "It's up to her," the doctor said. "The prognosis isn't good, but if she changes her lifestyle, she could have time. I wish we had a crystal ball to predict for you but we don't. Of course, she should get her things in order."

Worse than Monika had thought. The doctor spoke to her in the corridor, and when Monika went back to the room, her mother was laughing about something with her friend, Christa. It had to do with money, the time years ago she had been too broke to buy cigarettes and had scrounged for used butts in a café ashtray. The manager had thrown her out!

"You know," her mother said to Christa, "my daughter does very good work for a living. With art. Restoring order to the world."

"Yes, it's good," Christa said.

The job was more tedious than it looked. She'd been hired to go over lists that had already been gone over, to see if she could fill gaps. Any small trace she found—an auction record, a link to a suspect seller—was added to the online catalogue of work acquired in certain years, in case anyone wanted to make a claim. No claimants had appeared during her time at the museum.

"At least they pay you," her mother said. "I'm never going back to work if I don't have to. I can starve, I don't mind starving."

"Yes, you do," Christa said.

"I'm sick enough," her mother said, "to do whatever I want."

The day Monika took her home from the hospital, her mother had pinned her streaky hair into a twist and put on red lipstick. She wore a blouse and a trim skirt like a woman ready for a job interview she knew wouldn't go well. In the car Monika had ordered for them, her mother kept saying, "Oh, well, at least I'm going home."

On her lap Monika carried a cardboard bakery box. Her mother had complained she was going nuts from not smoking, and her friends had brought to the hospital great quantities of sweets to distract her. Jelly doughnuts, big chewy gingerbread cookies, poppy seed cake. Monika planned to set out a good tea with the leftovers when they got home.

"Oh," her mother said, when she walked through her own door, "it looks different."

"I cleaned up."

"I don't mean that." Her mother was settling herself onto the couch. "I have to get used to it again. I don't work anymore, I'm an invalid."

"A woman of leisure."

"Try not to condescend to me," her mother said.

Monika ignored her and set out the cakes. "I don't want you eating any of this," her mother said. "We have to save it for when Bruno comes."

In the hospital she'd introduced Bruno to all the nurses as Monika's father. As if they'd been a real couple; as if they'd had a far greater love than they ever had.

"You're going home soon anyway," her mother said. "To be in New York with your husband. Or didn't you leave him last year? I thought you left him."

"Stop it."

Her mother gave a dry laugh. Would it help her now if she had a man with her? Men hadn't been all that much help in her younger days, not as Monika remembered it. She wasn't about to find any new ones now, though you never knew with her.

"Look at you," her mother said. "Healthy and married."

"I never get sick. In New York everybody gets colds in winter and I don't even get a cold."

"I was always healthy too. I never took care of myself when I was young. I went and did what I wanted and I was lucky."

Monika had never thought of her mother as lucky.

"Never sick a day in my life. Nothing wrong with me till now."

"Just don't smoke."

"It's almost over," her mother said, slowly, with a rise in her voice. "What *is* it?"

She meant life. Did she expect Monika to answer this? Her mother was giving her a very long, direct gaze. And the question was not even a question but a complaint. So much trouble, and for what?

"You have more time, I think," Monika said.

Which was not an answer and made her mother very angry. "You don't know anything," she said. "You were always a bullshitter. You were. You always snuck off and lied to me."

"Of course," Monika said.

Her mother had started to drink a cup of tea and was nibbling on the piece of Obstkuchen she'd said she wasn't hungry for. She was wan and dull-skinned but she did look better now, didn't she?

"You weren't that bad a mother," Monika said.

Not too hard to say, but it startled her to see from her mother's face that she believed her.

Was that what she wanted, those words? You'd think she could have done a better job of it then. But people often wanted payment for what they only wished they'd done. Her mother did look happy now, soft and tender and gratified.

When Julian called, he said, "Don't get too settled in there. I mean in Berlin."

She imagined Julian in the room with her mother. Maybe it could have been all right now; he and her mother could have worked it out. Maybe.

"I wish you liked it better here," Monika said.

"Well, I don't."

"Bruno's disappeared again. Not that I blame him."

Her mother did blame him, of course. But would even a love much more substantial than Bruno's have been of any use? Monika didn't think so. People thought love was everything, but it could do so much and no more.

Could it save her sixty-one-year-old mother from heart disease? Could it stop wars, block floods, slow down hurricanes? Maybe *save* was the wrong way to look at it. Surely too much was asked of love.

Later that day Bruno sent her an email—*working hard for husband, calling in favors for Art Fair, one more person to talk to.* Monika decided it would be highly unwise to mention anything to Julian. She'd hate it if she had to untell him. All the same she was hit hard with disappointment when Bruno finally phoned her with the news that all his efforts (if he'd made any) had come to naught.

"It's too late, you know," Bruno said. "You should've started before."

Why do I let him con me? she thought. *And how many people have asked that question?*

"Your mother," he told her, just as Monika was sitting in the room with said mother, "is very proud to have a daughter who'll always take care of her. You should hear her go on."

"My mother just told me," Monika said, "that her favorite city in the world is Istanbul. Even though you ran off with an Italian while she was there. She says she got back at you later. And that you all made tons of money from whatever you bought in Turkey." Was it drugs, had her mother dealt drugs?

"We never made lots of money. No matter what she tells you. Your mother has never been rich," Bruno said. "Don't forget that."

"How could I?" Monika said.

And she did go to the bank twice before she left and took out enough to leave her mother an envelope with seventeen hundred euros in it. Not a lifesaving amount but it would help fill in the gaps and delays, since her mother had never been good at budgeting. "Just so you have cash on hand," Monika said.

"Oh!" her mother said. "This isn't because you're never coming back?"

Monika blushed from the wildness of this thought, which she hadn't even had. "No, no, I'll be back."

"I didn't think," her mother said, hugging her, "you would turn out so well!"

"Surprise, surprise."

"My own *Mausi*. You have enough money for you? You didn't give me too much? I know your husband isn't earning."

"No problem. Really," Monika said.

"Don't tell Bruno. He always borrows."

We will miss our good generous girl, Bruno wrote in his final message to her (he'd been told), *and hope you won't forget us. Say hello to your talented husband and guess what? The gallery owner who liked his work so much is very interested to see more.* Contact information fol-lowed—she only hoped it wasn't bogus. Julian would be happy about this, and he'd think it was her doing. She was coming home with a gift. She would have to tell him all the work she'd done to get it, how doggedly she had talked him up, how much the man admired the photos.

The night before she left, she and her mother got drunk on a bottle of herbal schnapps, which couldn't have been good for her mother's heart and made both of them giddy. It wasn't bearable to imagine that she might not see her mother again, this woman wearing red lipstick and laugh-ing about Angela Merkel's haircuts. They were parting on good terms, weren't they?

She was washing the dishes when she heard her mother grumble, "What a bitch you turned out to be. You couldn't even leave me just one. Was that too much to ask?" Monika had thrown out all the packs of cigarettes in the apartment, and now her mother had drunk enough to remember that she wanted a cigarette, why couldn't she have one?

Monika wanted to say, *You can go back to being a fuck-up when I'm gone,* as if that even needed saying. Instead she went out the door and down the stairs and around the corner, just before the Mini Markt closed, and she bought a pack of Marlboros for half of what they would've been in New York. On the walk home, she took out a single cigarette and threw the rest in a trash bin.

And when her mother took the offered cigarette and sat back in her chair to have Monika light it, she exhaled the smoke with much drama and said, "I knew you'd do it. I knew if I asked you right."

She might've been saying this fondly, but Monika felt taunted.

In the morning the schnapps put Monika on the plane with a hangover, and in her heavy-headed state, she spent the flight daydreaming of Julian. She was going home not only with desire (plenty of that) but also with relief at getting out of there, and was that heartless of her? A little.

When she walked through the door of their apartment in Bushwick, it struck her that she hadn't been sure, not entirely, that Julian would still be there. Here he was— was he taller?—in his black eyeglasses, his ancient gray T-shirt—the actual Julian. "Hey, girl," he said. He clung to her for a full minute, by way of greeting. Had he been worried?

"Back at last," she said.

"I can't believe you did that," he said later. "In the midst of everything else." He meant the alleged interest from a gallery in Berlin. It did seem to be a real gallery, one whose name he knew. He was not humble by nature but something like gratitude flowed from him. "One toe in the door," he said. She'd surprised him with a wifeliness he didn't imagine her having.

All from Bruno showing off. The part that puzzled

Monika was that anyone had listened to Bruno for a second. Favors owed, drugs shared? No way to know. Bruno had gone to some trouble for her, in his way. He had things to make up for, didn't he? There was more to be said for the power of regret than was often said.

The gallery owner wrote back at once—he admired the way Julian's work "combined commentary and lyricism" while it altered the perception of spaces. The phrases made Monika remember what she liked when she liked it.

Julian was so pleased. As he moved through their rooms, he kept coming back to touch her, on the shoulder, at the hip. She loved his hands on her. He hadn't been this glad to be around her since they'd first gotten back together, after she'd left. How very good it all was now, a good phase. Better than many. She was still waiting to tell him she'd dropped a chunk of their household budget on her mother.

Monika had not quite gotten over jet lag when she had her appointment with Lynnette, and it was a luxury to settle back into the chair with her eyes closed. They were a mess, her eyebrows. "Lot of work here," Lynnette said.

Monika explained the whole thing about where she'd been.

"Your mom's okay?"

"I don't know. You can't know."

Monika was about to complain of all she'd had to do in Berlin—the endless visits to the hospital, the pesky errands for her mother, the humoring of Bruno, the euros she'd been convinced to leave behind—but she decided not to. She had done all that willingly, hadn't she? What was the point if she hadn't done it with a willing heart?

Lynnette said, "My own mom's only forty-five, but it's a miracle she's not dead. Proof that God looks out for idiots."

"Mine could live forever under that theory," Monika said. Lynnette was dabbing on the soft wax with its oddly pleasant warmth. "You know what she said to me on the phone last night?"

Even Lynnette couldn't guess.

"If I moved back to Berlin without my husband I could get someone better to marry me."

"I thought you liked your husband."

"I do."

"Guess you weren't persuaded then."

"She'll try anything. Always has. My husband says it's her way of thanking me, this pressure to move back."

She'd been quite astonished that Julian could see it this way.

Had she fixed things with Julian now? Could that be done? That was the question asked every day, all over: *how much could ever be fixed?* To ask was to sound cynical. And yet people who heard about Monika's job always said what an excellent idea it was, return stolen art, return funds, do something.

Lynnette had now peeled off the wax and was on to the last bits of plucking, which she did with fierce swiftness.

"Julian will never leave New York, he just won't. Even if we're always broke," Monika said.

"Of course, I myself personally can't see living in Germany," Lynnette said. "With the Nazis."

Monika had already pointed out to Lynnette more than once that the war had been over for almost seven decades and the Nazi Party was illegal. But the worst facts dwarfed everything, didn't they; no explanation could hold ground against that history.

"You know what it would cost to move that far?" Lynnette said. "Hard to make big changes without cash. You tell your mother that."

Monika laughed. "She'll tell me to rob a bank then."

Who knew what her mother could ever ask for? Money took up a lot of room in her dreams, as it did in Lynnette's. The last-minute envelope Monika had handed her mother had caught her off guard—*what's this?* By now she might already be fretting there wasn't more in it. But at the moment she had been giddy and jubilant, relieved to be loved, properly startled, and Monika was glad to think of it.

"My brother," Lynnette said, "keeps saying he's saving his money. I'll believe it when I see it."

"He's young, right?" Monika said. "He can save later."

"Got a lot of years ahead of him," Lynnette said. "My big-shot brother."

Monika's eyebrows looked vastly better—what would she do without Lynnette? When she dug into her wallet to tip her, Monika almost gave her five euros by mistake. How odd it was to see it now, the bill with its engraving of a classical aqueduct, as if she'd been traveling between dimensions. "It's good money," Monika said.

"All money is good. But we take American here."

"I bet other people forget and slip you foreign coins. People who travel."

"I pity the fool," Lynnette said, "tries it on me."

Part III

8

I never liked Lynnette. I didn't even like the way she said my name, "Ray-n-a," too slow as if it were in quotes. How had Boyd ever liked her? I didn't actually ask him that—I had my own ideas, too many of them, and I didn't really want to know. She had her points, okay. But we weren't destined to be fans of each other.

I heard more Lynnette stories after I left my aunt's apartment and was back in the neighborhood. People said that for weeks she wouldn't stop talking on and on wherever she went. She bothered her friends with phone calls any time of day or night, left ranting voicemails. Did anyone have any idea how many bones Claude had broken in the crash? Did people know he had once memorized a whole chapter of some fantasy novel and everyone thought he was so dumb? Why did they think he had died really? The true reason?

In the next phase, she kept her mouth shut. She hung

out in the coffee shop where Boyd worked and sat drinking glasses of milk and saying nothing for hours. Boyd was able to get her to leave with intelligent coaxing, but some weeping and protest were involved on her part.

What saved her was the need for money. She had to move out of these spells of raging grief—in its manic and its icy stages—and remember how to feed herself. She had to go back to work in that salon and do whatever she did to women's eyebrows and she had to speak to people and make sense. Whatever they talked about in those places— TV stars' sex lives, weather trends, vegan diets—she was better off once she was doing it again.

I heard some of this from a woman in my building who used to go out with Maxwell and some other parts from a mother with a kid in Oliver's daycare group. The later reports made me less afraid of meeting Lynnette, but in fact I never saw her, even after Kiki returned and Oliver and I were resettled on our old block.

And now that my aunt was in New York again, at the end of her three weeks away, she kept calling me on the phone. "You can come back and stay any time, you know that," she said. "If you feel uncomfortable where you are. If you're afraid that what's his name—Boyd—is going to come bother you in any way."

"Boyd!" I said. "Why would he do that?"

And then Oliver had to start shrieking in the background. "Boyd's coming! When's Boyd coming?"

"He's not. He's not, not coming," I said.

But Oliver wouldn't stop; he got stuck inside this. "Boyd is too coming, you don't know anything," he said. "He wants to see us!" Oliver could shout very loud when he wanted.

"I don't think so," I said.

What did she mean, *bother me*? I'd only once had a boyfriend who was in any way abusive—Oliver's father, Kelvin—and I left him before Oliver was born. Nothing I said was going to make any difference to her.

"Put him to bed. I'll call you later," Kiki said.

"I'll have him calmed down in a minute."

"It's hard for kids to get it when things are over," my aunt said.

"He has to learn that," I said, with Oliver still making a racket. "Everyone has to learn that now."

In my apartment, I looked again for any of the cigarette money left behind. Who knew what hidden nooks some of those packs of bills might have just slipped down into? I was thinking I would send whatever money there was to Lynnette. *Here it is, it's yours.* A windfall of cash might remind her of better days. I told Oliver I was conducting an autumn cleanup, and he said, "You make it messier."

Claude used to always say he was planning to set his sister up in her own brow bar. He considered himself already very close to being filthy rich. All she needed was a lease on a storefront—eyebrows eternally! That was what she longed for, to be her own boss (she already bossed everyone), and a place like that could keep her going long after the initial investment was gone.

If I happened to find enough money, Lynnette would see, when the sum came to her, that I wasn't the person she had to hate. Her email address was on my computer, leftover from the invitation she'd sent for Claude's birthday party, and her home address was on the invite. I could put a check in the mail to her, simple as that, or I could send the money online by PayPal or something. I knew how to spell the woman's name.

I knew I was making this up, but it was an idea that did me good. I had no way on earth to undo what I wanted every day not to have done. Claude was never coming back. But here was something I could do—say what you will, money had the power to improve some of Lynnette's circumstances. Too bad there was no money.

When I went to get Oliver at daycare, I was early and I had to wait outside in the hall while they finished number puzzles. Waiting with me in the hallway was Tania, the mom who'd gone to high school with Maxwell and Boyd. She was looking perky, with petunia-pink lipstick. I had to say, "You hear any news about Maxwell?"

"He's still getting himself fixed up," she said, "but he'll be okay. That's what they say. They can fix him. He's staying with his sister in Albany, he'll be back."

"And how's Lynnette doing?" I didn't know I was going to say that.

"How up-to-date are you? You know the thing with the wrecked car? Which was in her name."

How smart of me not to let them put it in mine. It was not pleasant to have to picture the Taurus, with its dented silver finish and the rabbit doll Wiley had hung on the mirror for luck.

"You know it costs fifty dollars every day your car's in storage? Even if it's a wreck they can't move? They just keep charging you. And then they wanted her to pay them to haul it to some junk dealer," Tania said.

"What happened?"

"It went on much too long. They threatened her until the guys got it together to get money to help her. Boyd and some friends."

"There was cash in the car," I said. Was this stupid to utter?

"It walked away," she said. "Some cops got lucky. Or the towing crew. None of the guys was in a hurry to call to ask about it."

Everything up in smoke. Their theory had been very simple—buy cheap, sell fast. Wiley picking out expensive clothes for any female he was dating. Claude buying toys for his new girlfriend's kid. Boyd reading through apartment listings, for us. All that dreaming.

One of Oliver's teachers opened the classroom door just then, and we had to find our kids amid the clanging chairs and tables and the other restless four-year-olds. "Hey!"

Oliver said. "I'm going to count to a hundred for you. One two three four five six seven eight . . ." He did the whole thing.

All that night I was thinking about Claude. I was remembering the time he bought that toy piano for his girlfriend's kid. We all went to some discount store with him; we had to watch him look at the cartons of different keyboards. They wouldn't let him try any, just look. "Which you think is the best?" he said. He never even met the kid. Oliver had opinions, but at the cash register he started crying when he realized no one was letting him play with it; the box was staying closed. "Kid makes a lot of noise," Claude said. "Over nothing."

"Better get used to the noise," Boyd said.

"Jeshauna won't cry with me around," he said. He almost believed himself, too. It was a happy day. "Don't laugh *that* hard," he said to me.

In the meantime, Sabina, my friend, was excited about a new boyfriend, and why shouldn't she be? I made a full display of totally fake interest. She said he was one of the cooks at the restaurant where she worked. "It's worth it to sleep with him just for his mushroom risotto. Just kidding," she said. "We're only starting, we don't even know each other. That's always the best part, isn't it?"

All her skepticism was bullshit. She had nothing but hope.

"You'll find someone, too," she said. "No rush."

I hadn't had any dreams about Boyd in a while, and it was more than a month since we'd seen each other. When I was at my aunt's, I had terrible dreams of longing. Boyd in all his sudden particulars (there he was) would be coming closer, he'd be with me but not quite, and just before he reached for me, I'd wake up in that strange bed, gypped and cheated and ridiculous.

"It's okay if you're not actively looking yet," Sabina said. "But don't let any grass grow under your feet."

"Don't worry about my feet," I said.

Sabina was annoying me. I saw why, in older places, widows weren't supposed to marry until a decent period had passed since the death. Those were rules that made sense. But whose widow did I think I was? Boyd was alive and well. Claude wasn't even a relative. One had left me and one had died. I wasn't going around wailing to the world about my tangled mourning—it was my own business.

"In Turkey you have to know how to bargain," my aunt said over the phone. She was congratulating herself for getting a deal on her cable bill. She had threatened to change companies—"you always have to be willing to walk away"—and they had come down on her monthly rate.

Kiki was a more practical person than I was. "You manage fine," she said.

And then I made the mistake of telling my aunt I needed to raise money for something. "I know it's weird," I said. "But it's just that I have someone I want to send money to."

"Boyd?"

"Oh, no," I said.

"Men who need money are trouble," Kiki said.

"It's not for Boyd," I said. "You think everything is about men."

"I do not," Kiki said.

"It's for my friend, Lynnette," I said. "You don't know her."

"You must be a good friend," Kiki said.

I wondered if Kiki thought we were lovers, the way she said this. But, no, she was off on a riff about loyalty, how important it was. Fierce loyalty. "That's how the Kurds survived for two and a half thousand years, while the Hittites and the Phrygians died out. Communal loyalty. Did you know that?"

I didn't.

"Whatever you hear about Kurds, I've known some fine ones."

I hadn't heard anything.

"Oh," my aunt said, "I've been with Pat too much."

Was my aunt stuck in the past? I had a second of wondering whether, thirty-odd years from now, I was going to be muttering about high and low cigarette taxes. Was that what happened to old love, it turned into floating opinions and overcharged facts? I supposed I thought of

Osman and any others as built into the wall of my aunt,
like workers killed building the pyramids. Kiki would not
have liked this comparison. I thought my aunt was a great
example of someone who did fine living alone, but I didn't
want to be my aunt.

I had a lot of friends who didn't have TVs anymore, they
only watched programs on their computers, but Oliver
and I were huge fans of the big fat TV that landed in our
living room when Boyd started raking in cash. My whole
life I never worried enough about money, people said I was
careless about finances, but I could love objects. One thing
I was sure of: Boyd was never coming back for the TV. He
was a person who hated stingy gestures, who liked open-
handedness and no looking back. Had I learned anything
from him?

In his early days at the diner, Boyd came home doing
sarcastic impressions of all the customers who counted out
tips in pennies. Nothing more pathetic than leaving pennies on the table. But then Wiley was always a big tipper,
wherever he went, so it wasn't everything.

I knew how I was going to raise the money for Lynnette. I
was going to sell the one thing of value I had, which was
the carpet that my aunt had given me. Unless it wasn't
worth enough to sell, which was certainly possible.

I did what anyone would do; I looked online. I pulled

up ads, I looked at eBay and 1stdibs and even Sotheby's.
I thought I knew what kind it was—my aunt always said
Kula, which was a place—and some of the rugs that came
up under *Kula* looked like mine and some didn't at all.
Selling for nineteen thousand dollars, selling for a hun-
dred dollars, best offer. Depending on what?

Mine was big, which was a good thing. Beautiful, of
course—brown and blue and a pale shrimpy yellow—with
a diamond medallion in the center and border designs of
clovers for luck and what Kiki had once told me were gold
scales, to measure sins and good deeds for the next world.
How perfect. The carpet wasn't new, obviously, but I had
no idea how old or how many knots per square inch or any
of the other crap I read about.

I folded it up and took it to a rug assessor. Google
knew where they were. I picked a guy in the West Thirties
I thought wouldn't be too fancy, but he was fancy enough,
white-haired and elegantly bossy. His shop was just aisles
of rugs, in piles as tall as he was. He unfurled mine on a
table, stared at it, stroked the nap, looked at the underside.
"Where did you get this?" A girl with tattoos like me.

It turned out to be in very good condition for how old
it was, which was older than it looked. Maybe 1900, no
moth holes, no worn spots. Faded, but natural dyes did
that, and natural was good. Did I know the golden yellow was from buckthorn? "For insurance," he said, "you
could put maybe five thousand if you want."

I let out a little gasp of surprise, and I realized I hadn't
loved the rug enough. It was like the nerdy kid in the class

who becomes a movie star; you have to say you always knew he was cool.

Oliver liked to roll his trucks over the pattern of the carpet, but I didn't think we would miss it so much. Kiki would be insulted and disappointed in me when she heard. I would have to block out a story about the glories of friendship, my loyalty. My friend Lynnette, she's had a hard time with her family, I can't begin to tell you, very bad situation, a friend has to do things, if you knew her, you'd understand.

So I took some photos and listed it on eBay for $4,900 and waited. No response the first day. I kept checking. I edited my description, added that the town of Kula was an important rug-making center, a phrase I took from the masses of info online.

At work people told me I looked less tired, more up-beat. "Staying at your aunt's place was good, wasn't it?" one of the techs said. "She must have a super apartment."

If I was better, it was because I had a plan, I was in the midst of getting something done. For a change. The tech spoke to me as he was walking a dog out to its owner in the waiting area, an old black Lab named Scuffy whom I'd seen many times. The animal was heading toward his human with simple dog glee, pulling at the leash, openmouthed and smiling, and I thought how life was clearer with a goal.

•

How long was I going to have to wait? After a week, two people were "watching" my item but no offers. I wasn't going any lower. Wasn't I? I didn't know what I was doing.

Of course, I saw the lunacy of acting as if money could fix what had happened, like tribesmen paying for a death by offering so many sheep. I didn't tell anybody what I was doing so no one talked me out of it. It was a secret vigil I was keeping, a faith I invented. At work I checked my phone all the time—the screen as closet shrine. I sort of chanted to it, too—I heard myself say "come on" and "not yet?" and "oh, please." It was no odder than the pleading many people did; I wasn't begging a lover but an absent buyer, a stalling wallet.

I lowered the price to $4,800, why not, and that very night at 11:52 p.m. a message appeared that really, actually said someone bought the rug. It was a woman from Augusta, Maine—she was paying me seventy-five dollars to ship it to her—and the total sum would soon appear in my PayPal account, minus fees to eBay and PayPal. A done deal, here it was. Sold! What if I changed my mind, what if I never sent the carpet at all? I'd had it since Oliver was a baby. My aunt gave it to me.

I went through a very bad night, but by morning I remembered that selling the carpet was half of my idea—the other half was getting the money to Lynnette and would be much more pleasurable. I had to focus on the higher goal, the longer view. By the time I went to pick up Oliver that evening, the rug was gone. I'd moved the furniture off it, vacuumed it, folded and rolled it and wrapped it in plastic, and taken it to UPS. Oliver said, "We have wood on the floor," and began jumping and tapping with his shoes, which he knew he wasn't supposed to do.

Lynnette wasn't yelling at people these days, but she was still Lynnette.

It was all too possible that she'd tear up a check or delete an email if she saw my name anywhere near it. She had her principles and her fury and she was more than capable of raging refusal, even when it meant cutting off her nose to spite her face. She'd walk around without a nose, no problem.

My first idea had been to just send her mystery cash in the mail, unsigned—put a wad of bills in a big envelope, put it inside a gift box with a nice scarf or something, and take it to the post office. The mail was really very reliable these days—slow in New York, but things didn't get lost. Didn't our tax forms always arrive at the IRS? They did.

I had to send the money fast before I spent it. There were things I wanted to buy, things I needed—an iPad for Oliver, great shoes I saw in a store window, a better phone. Just this, just that, very tempting, and once I started chipping away, the dollars would shrink to nothing. My customer had thirty days on her money-back guarantee, but I decided (somehow) that I could take my chances after a week. A risk was better than a total loss. I couldn't stay like this any longer, caught in the middle, snagged.

I did know Lynnette, and she was famous for loving a particular kind of chocolates, caramels with smoked salt, which she said were better than sex (what a tacky cliché); she'd be glad to get them in the mail. They came in packs of six, so I bought three of those and wrapped them, along with a large plastic baggie full of hundred-dollar bills, in nice gold wrapping paper and put this big lump inside a large padded envelope. I wrote the candy company's address in Seattle as the return address.

I was all charged up, waiting in that long fucking line at the post office. I was holding so much cash—all those bills in my package sending off burning rays, smoking in their own heat. What if someone in line grabbed it from me and ran off? Oh, who was I kidding, it wasn't that vast a fortune anyway. And money was nothing, money wasn't everything. But I had made a great errand out of this money. My sacred padded brown envelope, labeled and stapled and taped, getting sweaty in my hands, overstuffed with meaning. I had to wait till the next postal clerk would take it from me.

For days I looked for Tania at Oliver's daycare—who else could tell me about Lynnette? I showed up early, I lingered as long as I could, no Tania in sight. What if I never heard any news at all? Why had I done this? Not for gratitude (I'd given up that part). For my own private mind. My aunt always said that was what you had at the end of it all.

When Tania appeared, finally, at the end of the week,

she said, "I guess you heard—it's so insane! Lynnette and the Isaiah thing."

The what? Lynnette had understood at once that her old boyfriend, Isaiah, who had first given her such candy, was behind the anonymous envelope. For a long time he'd been unfindable (hadn't she tried to trail him online?) and he seemed to need to stay that way, but he was providing for her. "Providing big-time," Tania said.

And what a change it had made in Lynnette. "You wouldn't know her if you saw her. She was never what we'd call a smiley girl. But now she goes around blessing everybody. I know, it's horrifying."

Look what love had done, even if it hadn't done it.

"She sent some bucks to her crazy mother in Philadelphia. And now she's moving back there, so she can set up a brow bar. I guess it's cheaper there. Well, anywhere is cheaper than here."

Isaiah was the light on her horizon, the joy in her illusion. So Boyd hadn't even been the one.

"She claims to know how to run a business," Tania said. "Big surprise to me."

Love was lifting her higher. Candy in the mail and she was ready to rule.

"She can do it," I said. "All sorts of idiots do it."

Claude would've been very pleased, I heard myself think. He and Lynnette would've been partying all over town, hitting the clubs. I hoped she had other people to celebrate with. Maybe Boyd, maybe he was toasting her right now, maybe Maxwell, if he was back. Lynnette would be holding forth about the importance of proper eye beauty, its contribution to global progress.

I had done what I wanted, which was a great thing, and I was mostly pretty delirious, but also confused. What if Isaiah turned up one day and let slip that it wasn't from him at all? What if, what if. She would still have gotten the money, and she'd have her business up by then. Lynnette would never guess it was from me either—I wouldn't be on her list. Maybe she'd decide it was from Boyd.

People always went for the romantic interpretation; you couldn't blame them for that. What they felt most strongly seemed most true. But other forces were operating in the world. Not just sex, but the armies of the righteous, battling on. I was the dispenser of blood money, the phantom bookkeeper. With an identity like that, fat chance anyone was going to uncover me.

I hadn't meant to nourish Lynnette by feeding her false information, but she might live to a ripe old age under the glow of what she believed about Isaiah. However people's eyebrows looked fifty years from now, she could be the gabby proprietor telling stories about the clever way her old lover, who never forgot her, had set her up in life.

No one knew the real story but me. I wanted to tell Boyd. He would think better of me if he knew; it would cause him to look back at our time together and see me differently.

He would remember our bad spots and think I had been
more generous than he realized—that my grouchiness had
come from being a good mother, my crabby remarks from
real worry. And my tenderness in bed had not been that of
a shallow person. I wanted him to find out who had sent
the money. I had my vanity.

I hadn't told anyone. Aunt Kiki believed that I listened
too much to other people, that that was the danger of being young. She was in favor of self-sufficiency, her and
Marcus Aurelius. I wasn't very attracted to any of this,
but I was keeping my mouth shut now in some kind of
imitation of it. I wasn't telling Kiki either.

But of course Kiki found out about the rug. Oliver told her
on the phone, he said his mother had thrown out the rug
he liked to play on, she was always doing things like that.
"I didn't throw it out," I had to say. "I sold it. I wanted the
money for my friend. I hope you're not mad."

"When I gave you that rug," my aunt said, "it was to
do whatever you wanted with. What kind of gift would it
be otherwise?"

"I got a good price," I said. "eBay is good. My friend,
the thing is, she was really in a bad way. Bad as it gets."

"I hope she's better," my aunt said. "I'm sure it meant
a lot to her that you helped."

"She says she'll never forget this."

"Well, she won't. These things stay. Maybe she'll help
you someday."

It was a little alarming to think of being helped by Lynnette. I'd have to be pretty wrecked and ruined. Maybe she could rescue me if I made an especially bad choice in a boyfriend. She could come swooping in and give him a piece of her mind, clear him out. "You listen to *me*," she'd say.

"I had it appraised," I said. "If you ever need money, you could go to this place." I had no real idea how much money my aunt had, though I had sometimes wondered.

"I kept the Kurdish one," my aunt said. "Well, you know my rug. They're much more popular now, the Kurdish patterns. Not so formal. It's worth more."

"Would you ever sell it?"

"Of course not," my aunt said. "You know that."

Oliver was still complaining in the background about how he needed a rug, his truck had no roads to play on, and nobody cared that he didn't have it. "You could get him a cheap one at Kmart," my aunt said. "That's what you should have."

There was a rumor that Lynnette had decided not to start any business after all but was going to buy a marble tombstone for Claude instead. I had no idea what gravestones cost, but this was a terrible idea, and only Lynnette could have thought of it, unless maybe her mother put her up to it. I heard about it from Angie, the girl in my building who'd once dated Maxwell. She was standing by the mailboxes in our hallway when she told me. "It's just throwing the money away," she said. "You think Claude really would've wanted some big hunk of rock? I do not think so."

Maybe he would have; I couldn't begin to say. I thought the dead were forever separate from us—that was what it meant to be dead. Lost to the living, not sending word. My father once told me that after his mother died when he was twelve, he always got angry if his father announced what she would've wanted him to do. "You don't know!" he'd say, when they both knew his father was making good guesses. My dad hated his father speaking for her, as if she were a puppet, as if he couldn't even honor the silence of the dead.

I hated thinking of Lynnette giving all the money to some cemetery. I hadn't sacrificed my aunt's great carpet for *that*. That wasn't what I meant at all. I knew I didn't get to choose; that was the whole point of sacrifice. But couldn't anyone stop her?

Boyd stopped her. Maxwell had just moved back into his old apartment, with Boyd in residence and taking care of Maxwell while he hobbled around on a crutch. Angie said the big scar on his face didn't look as bad as it might've, Maxwell could carry it off. Boyd and Maxwell together had paid a little trip to Lynnette's current place of work, Brow Central or whatever the fuck it was. They barely got as far as the receptionist, who wasn't so nice either, but they were politely leaving a note when Lynnette came out right at that moment. "Hello, beautiful," Boyd said.

"Bless your hearts," she said.

She was taking her lunch break, and, sure, she'd have a bite with them. So over tacos Boyd talked about life and death. What happened when a person died was that it turned you toward what was serious. When someone in the neighborhood (they'd grown up with this) poured out a Colt 45 on the ground for a dead friend, that was a serious moment. Claude had only been twenty-four, not a complete life, he died at the start of it, doing his work. The best way to remember Claude was for Lynnette to go on with her work. She was so good at it, everybody said that. Claude always bragged about her, he hoped to finance her someday. If you asked him, he would say she was a natural businesswoman too. And Claude really wouldn't have wanted any fucking rock.

What could she do but start crying and agree with them? Maxwell added that he'd help her with all the money calculations for her salon if she wanted help. Maxwell the mastermind.

I didn't trust her to stick with it, but Angie said that Maxwell was going to Philly with her to look at storefront rentals. He was hopping right on the bus, crutch and all, and close to four hours on a cheap-o-ride with no shocks wasn't going to be any picnic for him. No, Boyd wasn't going, Angie said. He couldn't leave the state, which I'd forgotten.

When I went to work that afternoon, I thought of Maxwell. He'd been in the hospital for three weeks, drugged, damaged, broken, all banged up, and then at his sister's, healing slowly. Everybody said he was a good sport about his crutch and claimed to be coming up with new dance moves. I imagined him directing Boyd from the sofa, telling him what kind of beer to bring him, what kind of chips to go out and buy, and Boyd saying, "Yeah, boss," handling it in his own way.

I hadn't even thought about Maxwell, because I could just about stand to think whatever I did. Where I sat at my desk at the veterinary clinic, we sometimes heard an animal yelping or crying—not often but sometimes—and these were terrible sounds, and the appalling part was having to sit there without getting up to rush to the animal. The vets were back there, nobody needed me, but the sounds didn't just slip by.

Maxwell had been the one with the idea to move cigarettes up from Virginia and he was probably working already on another idea. Angie said, "He's been trying to get more from the trucker's insurance company. Who knows? Maybe that'll pay off." I'd had secret fantasies of popping by the apartment to see Boyd, just showing up, but I wasn't paying any surprise visits if Maxwell was there. Nobody else was ranting like Lynnette, but I didn't see Maxwell jumping with joy at the sight of me. If he could jump at all.

My comfort (if you could call it that) was to imagine Maxwell advising Lynnette on the right storefront to rent. She could decorate any hole-in-the-wall to make it look good, but she had to pick a youthful neighborhood. Old people didn't give a fuck about their eyebrows. Kiki's were all grown out; even my mother didn't do much with hers. People in their twenties, myself included, thought they carried their lives in their looks. Even now, though I wasn't ready, I hoped for all the men on the block to love me when I walked out the door.

I wondered if Lynnette had beauty advice for Maxwell and his scar. Rub this on your face or that. Maxwell wouldn't want any conversation about it at all, I'd think. He'd want it ignored—his business, his to take as it was. His own skin.

In the reception area where I sat, the veterinarians had a bulletin board, photos of cats needing homes and ads from dog walkers and trainers. One of the cards from a trainer said, *New Puppy? Love Is Not Enough.* This was about dogs needing to be taught how to live with humans, but I always thought of it as a more universal warning, a reminder of the limits, a bit of truth from the roughest frontier.

My aunt said, "How is your friend doing? I hope she's better."

"Much better," I said. "She's starting her own business."

Aunt Kiki probably didn't think capitalism was a happy ending, but she made allowances for other people. She'd been a maid once herself.

"Were you still cleaning houses," I said, "when you were with Hernando?" I did remember Hernando, who'd been nice to me.

"Oh, no," she said. "I was out of that before you were born. I had another boyfriend then."

How busy my aunt had been.

"Do you miss your old lovers?"

Where did that come from? I knew where.

"Well, I always say I still love Osman." She did always say it, as if it were an ordinary fact easily absorbed into ongoing life. "Why would I stop?"

How logical my aunt could sound. What she meant, I thought, was that she didn't have to stop, because she was Kiki. She could manage both sides without too much trouble, the old love, fading fast but never gone, and the rest of her life that went on without it just fine.

"Of course," Kiki said, "you always remember the bad parts. He didn't think much about what I wanted. He assumed I'd go wherever he went. He refused to even visit New York. But I try to be fair to him in my head."

Nobody talked as much as Kiki did about the possibility of fairness. Of course, she had time and distance, years and miles, she wasn't in the thick of things. But all that fairness made her calmer, even I knew that.

Oliver had run into a little trouble at the daycare center when he balked about naptime, refused to lie down. "I'd love a chance to take a nap," I told him. He was complaining about stupid rules on our walk home, stupid stupid, when he stopped all of a sudden and shrieked, "There's Boyd! It's Boyd, hey!"

It was Boyd all right. He was in a black T-shirt and low-slung jeans, ambling along 125th Street, looking good. Oliver ran up and tackled him around the knees. "Whoa," Boyd said. "How you doing, my man?"

"We're fine," I said. Not that he'd asked about me. He and I weren't hugging each other either, nothing like that. "How are things?" I said. "Tell me how Maxwell is."

"Doing pretty good. He might walk okay sometime but they're not saying definitely."

"Everybody else okay?"

"Wiley's getting married," he said. "I know, I know, who'd guess? To the woman he was holed up with someplace for days while we were waiting for him to show up to drive the car. He says it's true love. Really, he says that."

My first thought was that Wiley, that shithead, was giving love a bad name.

The man didn't have a sincere bone in his body. But maybe I had it backward. Maybe love was raising him up, turning him around, starting him over.

"I guess that's good news," I said. I didn't say: *If he hadn't met her, Claude would still be around.* It did no good to unknot and rewind everything that way, I knew that.

Boyd said, "Could last. Nobody knows about these things."

Oh, were we going to have a talk about love? I stood looking at Boyd, trying to read his familiar face, while Oliver was starting to climb his leg like a tree.

"Nobody does know," I said. "Oliver, take it easy. Sometimes things continue underground."

"That they do."

"You think so?"

"Not everything gets acted out in this life," he said. "*Underground* is a good word."

I was enormously flattered. We agreed about this thing. Buried love. Its eternal zombie life.

"I always think I'm going to live to be very old," I said.

"I bet you do," he said. "And do it well."

"And you too, I wish you that." It was a meaningless conversation about love.

"Got a long time ahead of us," he said. "People living to be a hundred these days."

Till rivers all run dry. We were making great vows without the trouble of having to live with each other. But we were making them, standing on high ground to look down at the passage of time, years unfolding in the mortal valley below us.

I wasn't going to look that good when I was a hundred. I knew that wasn't the point, for me to worry how he might see me, if he could see.

"A hundred what?" Oliver said. "Can I have a hundred dollars?"

"Sure, right away," I said. "You still at the diner, Boyd?"

"Place couldn't go on without me."

I laughed, of all things to do. He couldn't guess how much I'd missed him. Maybe he could. There was no hope of ever being with him again—not a particle of

likelihood—so why was I so gone with joy at the sight of
him? There I was, smiling away.

Oliver said, "Did you know I hate naps?"

"I didn't know," Boyd said. "I'm so glad you told me."
He was hoisting Oliver up to stand on his shoes (Oliver
crowed) while Boyd walked him around in giant steps, the
way he used to. Just to remind me why I liked him better
than any other man in the world.

So everybody was going to Wiley's wedding. I heard this
from Tania a week later, outside the classroom where
we'd both dropped our kids off in the morning. "It's just
a city hall thing," Tania said. "But they're having a party
at somebody's that night." No one was set against Wiley
the way people were set against me. Same old Wiley. I was
pretty cut up about this.

"What's she like?" I said.

"Very pretty. I only met her for a second and she was
hanging on Wiley's neck like a boa constrictor."

"The man could use some choking," I said.

I heard how this came out, beyond bitchy, and Tania
looked startled.

"Well, he's getting strangled with love," I said, a very
lame do-over on my part. I was trying in some ridiculous
way to sound more like my aunt.

"I might go to the party," Tania said.

•

When Boyd was at Rikers, I came with Oliver to see him one day when we had to wait for hours. A fight had broken out somewhere and one section was under lockdown or maybe they all were, I didn't know. Anyway Oliver and I were stuck on a bench in a room that had a soda machine and a clock and maybe ten other worn-down visitors. I was supposed to meet Sabina for supper and I couldn't tell her how late (getting later by the minute) I'd be. My phone, my watch, my purse, Oliver's dinosaur, were all in a locker we couldn't get to, and we couldn't turn back even if we wanted. I had to keep Oliver occupied. I didn't have a pen or a pencil or a shred of paper. "I spy with my little eye," I said, "something blue. What is it?"

Oliver was not impressed. "That man's dungarees," he said. "So what?"

I goaded him into finding two more blue things— the guard's uniform, the paint on a doorframe—but he wasn't playing after that. "This is boring," he decided to inform me.

"Pretend you're a famous person," I said, "and I have to guess who you are." Was this too advanced for him?

"Okay, okay."

Living or dead? Living. Boy or girl? Boy. Grown-up or kid? Grown-up. Not on TV, not in movies, not in video games. Not in a story they read in daycare. Would everybody in the world know him? Yes. Was it the president? No. Did everybody in the world like him? Yes, yes. I was going to guess Jesus, in case Hector's family had sneaked that in. "You know," he said. "Boyd!"

Well, of course, what person would we wait for all day
like this but the king of the world?

"I really didn't guess," I said. "You're so smart."

When I told this to Boyd later, I tried to do it in a way
that didn't make fun of Oliver. It made the day so much
better. Boyd said, "I'd never guess either." Oliver thought
this was the funniest thing he'd ever heard, Boyd not
guessing himself.

In October, I got an email that came from Maxwell. *Best
Brow Bar in Philly Now Open*, the subject line said. I must
have been on his mailing list. I was dazzled by the words, a
vision from my head turned real suddenly. As if a language
I only spoke to myself was now being muttered all around
me. The email showed a brick wall painted spring-green
with a gold-framed mirror, a glass dressing table, a big
Boston fern on a stand. Welcome to the salon.

You could click the menu to read a list of services, and
you could see a photo of someone's perfect eyebrow. There
was a bio of Lynnette, detailing her long service in the chic
venue of Midtown New York and her passion to bring her
skills back to the town of her youth. Customers who came
on opening day could enjoy a glass of bubbly to hail the
new arrival.

The bio made Lynnette sound happy and triumphant,
so it was great reading for me. She'd be wearing some fabulous outfit at the opening, something sexy and shimmer-
ing, with slashes in the fabric and fringes. After one drink

she'd probably be blessing everybody. She might make a speech about hard times and getting back on her feet and thank the special people she needed to thank, Maxwell and Boyd and somebody she couldn't name. "Miracles happen. Every one of you has to believe," she would say. Someone might start to whisper and laugh at this, and Lynnette would say, "Cut it. I'm right." Her crazy mother would toast to big, big success. I was making this up but it gave me great pleasure, and it probably wasn't all that far from whatever happened. Claude would've been so glad to see all of it. Look at that now, he would've said to me, I knew it all along.

ACKNOWLEDGMENTS

I want to thank Myra Goldberg as ever for her astute and essential advice and her patience in reading. I also owe great thanks to Andrea Barrett, Kathleen Hill, Margarite Landry, and Chuck Wachtel. I am grateful to my editor, Dan Smetanka, and everyone at Counterpoint, and to my agent, Geri Thoma, and Andrea Morrison. Special thanks to Levent Kocabaş, Seref Ufuk Altug, and Aydın Can for teaching me about Turkey. And thanks to the MacDowell colony for a residency during the writing of this book.

Portions of this novel have appeared previously in magazines. The first chapter appeared under the title "About My Aunt" in *Tin House* and was included in *The O. Henry Prize Stories 2015* and *The Best American Short Stories 2015*. The fourth chapter appeared under the title "Coverage" in the *Colorado Review*.

Joan Silber is the author of eight books of fiction. *Improvement* was the winner of the National Book Critics Circle Award for Fiction and the PEN/Faulkner Award. It was listed as one of the year's best books by the *Washington Post,* the *Wall Street Journal, Newsday,* the *Seattle Times* and *BBC Culture.* In 2018 she also received the PEN/Malamud Award for excellence in the short story. Her previous book, *Fools,* was longlisted for the National Book Award and a finalist for the PEN/Faulkner Award. Other works include *The Size of the World,* finalist for the LA Times Fiction Prize, and *Ideas of Heaven,* finalist for the National Book Award and the Story Prize. She lives in New York and teaches at Sarah Lawrence College and in the Warren Wilson MFA Program.